COURAGE

Coraje: perra heroe de la frontera

WEBB & FRANCISCA SPRAGUE

BALBOA.
PRESS
A DIVISION OF HAY HOUSE

Balboa Press books may be ordered through booksellers or by contacting:

Balboa Press
A Division of Hay House
1663 Liberty Drive
Bloomington, IN 47403
www.balboapress.com
1 (877) 407-4847

Because of the dynamic nature of the Internet, any web addresses or
links contained in this book may have changed since publication and
may no longer be valid. The views expressed in this work are solely those
of the author and do not necessarily reflect the views of the publisher,
and the publisher hereby disclaims any responsibility for them.

The author of this book does not dispense medical advice or prescribe the use
of any technique as a form of treatment for physical, emotional, or medical
problems without the advice of a physician, either directly or indirectly. The
intent of the author is only to offer information of a general nature to help
you in your quest for emotional and spiritual well-being. In the event you use
any of the information in this book for yourself, which is your constitutional
right, the author and the publisher assume no responsibility for your actions.

Any people depicted in stock imagery provided by Thinkstock are
models, and such images are being used for illustrative purposes only.
Certain stock imagery © Thinkstock.

Printed in the United States of America.

ISBN: 978-1-4525-1531-1 (sc)
ISBN: 978-1-4525-1533-5 (hc)
ISBN: 978-1-4525-1532-8 (e)

Library of Congress Control Number: 2014909279

Balboa Press rev. date: 06/19/2014

CONTENTS

AN OPEN LETTER
TO MY GRANDCHILDREN

Dear Damaris and Julia,

Did you ever watch Courage sleep or stop and smell the wind? Did you notice how sometimes she just stands there or looks to be running or making little sounds? Like us, dogs remember, and I imagine sometimes their memories of adventures are good – sometimes bad – and sometimes nightmares.

This story is really two stories: The first is the story we all share. It's a history of our dog Courage, your family, Nana and me and you. Damaris and Courage were puppies together, and Julia came along a little bit later. Ours is the greater story of a mid life Mexican and late life American marriage and family.

We live in La Frontera which is an area legally 40 miles north of the border between Mexico and the United States and culturally anywhere from just north of the border fence on an exclusive golf club or thousands of miles north to inner city Chicago.

The second is a story told to us by Courage. A heroic adventure in La Frontera, she shares her story in a manner similar to that of author Jack London. Her adventure is of herself, hero dog– a little wolf who saves her humans from the clutches of some narco traficantes. Her adventure reflects the ecological, political and criminal realities that describe the issues of the borderlands along the American Southwest and Mexico's Northwest for those of us who live in La Frontera.

Memories reflect a reality in ways far more important than what we do in our every day lives. In memories we don't need to worry about time or place. Free from these restraints, we can look toward the future and what we want to do and how and what we want to be. Courage shows dog like qualities of loyalty, persistence, bravery and friendship– these aspects of her character triumph over the distinctly human qualities of violence and treachery.

A little magic, spirituality, humor and a shape -shifting angel who just loves beans help us along her journey's way.

An old man, I share with you the vision I've lived and the reality I've experienced. Drifting toward the sleep that surrounds all our lives, I regard it a privilege to write of our history and our pet's heroic vision.

Be well and love, Grandpa.

At the end of the letter, Julia asked,

"But why a dog to tell a story of La Fonterra? Why not us- why not a human? A reporter? A migra-border patrol officer or even a narco traficante?"

"For any number of reasons," I replied:

- *Anonymity. La Frontera can be a very dangerous place. It's doubtful that a human could survive the trip without being recognized and murdered. A dog? A beautiful Siberian husky whom everybody wants to pet? Nobody would notice.*

- *Dogs can survive in the wild. Dogs are stronger, faster and tougher than humans– in particular our Husky and her best friend Tuma, a Malamute. These dogs are one evolutionary step away from their ancestor the Grey Wolf. The only enemy of wolves is man.*
- *Dogs do not have time for calculated response. Theirs is a world where they must instantly decide who is friend or who is enemy or who is to be eaten or who will eat you.*
- *With senses of hearing and smell far superior to humans, dogs live in a different world simply because they hear and smell things we humans don't. This sensory information plus the need to rely on instantaneous intuitive responses allows dogs to be open to things humans would miss– yes, like angles and devils."*

Damaris, the older sister and family administrator then asked, "Grandpa, will people really believe our dog's trip? Even though we've made the much of the same trip, can we prove it?"

In the past I told doubters, "Si quieres preguntar, Preguntarle a la perra" – but this time I've written detailed descriptions of Courage's journey from Indio to the narco's hideout just outside El Dorado, Mexico. But better take the bus to Culiacan –even going south, The Beast, the north –south railroad, is too dangerous. Just follow the directions.

"OK enough questions," I continued, "I'm out of answers. My suggestion is to be like our dog Courage: Be still and listen, smell and feel the wind. The answers and God are in it.

COURAGE: MUCH MORE THAN LEASH CANDY...MUCH MORE.

"Courage?" Interesting name for a dog: More resonant than brave. Closer to valor – a Spanish cognate. Do I have courage? Actually I am quite cautious. But when it comes to my pack –wolf or human, I will endure pain, hunger, thirst and even give my life.

Is that courage?

Named for <u>Courage the Cowardly Dog</u>, I remain at age 10- about 70 in human years- a beautiful and charming Siberian husky, spoiled by loving humans and admired by all my neighbors. First cousin of the feared Grey Wolf, I remain the little girl wolf - la lobita- the dog with a smile and a tail held high who prances and dances through her days.

Like humans and other animals, maybe even cats, my life is one of routines: Up in the morning for a walk, time to move my bowels, then home to food and a nap. And pretty much the same in the evening. Sure, life can liven up with a tummy rub or a vacation run in the beach, but that's the exception and far from the rule.

Sometimes, however, life intrudes and there is an event – a singularity that defines a life and brings meaning to existence that is more than just watching Dad pick up my poop in a plastic bag. Mine was the time when I became Hero Dog and saved my humans from some dreadful narco traficantes. The whole adventure took the better part of March 2010, but, although a short period of time, it was an experience that continues to define my life.

My adventure remembers La Frontera- my desert home, the borderlands between Mexico and the United States. An American-made double-sided wall snakes across a continent gashing the countryside and separating, people, families, jobs and cultures shared by Mexico and the United States. As dangerous as it is dynamic, La Frontera defines the narcotics trade that costs 15,000 Mexican lives a year supplying American's insatiable desire for drugs.

As I stand still and smell the wind, hearing sounds and smelling smells that humans can only imagine, memories come flooding back. Again I am Courage, Hero Dog of the Borderlands. My heart beats wolf and my Husky soul sings virtue as I jump the border to save my humans from a bogus kidnapping attempt.

Greater Love has no one than that he
lay down his life for his friends.
John 15: 13

CHAPTER 1

KIDNAPPED

Foolishly – very foolishly I might add – Mom and Dad left for vacation without me. I tried everything to keep them from going – but they felt they had to go and the best I could hope for was that they would miss me. That was until I learned that they had been kidnapped.

With news of the kidnapping I began my journey to save my humans from some horrible narco traficantes. I sprang into action and began the dangerous journey south through the perils of the Coachella Valley Desert, Mexicali and onto Sinaloa. A lonely trip and very dangerous – you had better believe it. Tired, sick and frightened, I woke from a fitful night's sleep by the Salton Sea to find a giant coyote less than 10 feet away -150 pounds of red eyed ferocity –with me on his mind. I would fight to the death...my inner wolf would not go easy.

For some reason, Dad loves to quote Shakespeare. And his favorite quote is from *The Tempest* and it goes something like this, "We are such stuff as dreams are made on, and our little life is surrounded by a sleep." Maybe he thinks he's Prospero.

Maybe he is; maybe he's not, but he doesn't understand when dreams become visions and visions become adventures and adventures become quests.

Now, listen to my story, and you'll agree that, while beautiful, I'm much more than just Leash Candy.

***

Indio, CA., Monday, March 1, 2010

My humans are going to leave me, I realized most unhappily. How could they leave their Beautiful Dog – everybody calls me that. For good reason – I am *Perra Bonita*. But they are still going to leave me.

I've tried everything: I rolled on my back, very modestly I might add with my tail between my legs- Dad never resist that move and always gives me a tummy rub – yes, he gave me a tummy rub all right, but he's still going to leave me. I even employed the nuclear option –the Hang Dog Look – gets them every time. I almost made Dad cry, but still no luck.

OK, I know I can be bossy – I prefer alpha: Yes, I always demand the front seat in the car when we go driving, and I know that my leash has two ends. But I also feel responsibility for the well being of my humans. Now, who's going to look after them when I'm not there; they're getting old and Goodness only knows what kind of trouble they could get into.

"Corazon, Sweetheart," I heard Mom say to Dad, "you know we can't take Courage with us. Mazatlan and Sinaloa are too far away to drive and besides that with all the gangas – not very safe. You yourself have said we can't take her on the plane. If we even got her on the plane we'd have to put her in a cage in the baggage compartment and risk her life with extremes of heat and cold. Imagine her in Sinaloa – chasing and probably catching everybody's chickens and fighting with the other dogs –remember how she gets them all riled up when you take her for a walk in Mexicali? And our darling pooch would most assuredly catch fleas – can you imagine how indignant her majesty would be with pulgas? No, darling, you know we have to leave her. We'll be back."

"Mexico...Shmexico ...Sinaloa. ...Shminiloa... Mom can be so hard; I almost got Dad – at least I made him tear up," I thought as I resigned myself to human betrayal. "Now Abuelita, my Grandma, is supposed to babysit for me while they're gone. She calls me Burra – Stupid? – I think not. She's even older than Dad –as hard to believe as that may be. Perhaps I'm supposed to babysit her."

What about the rest of La Familia? There are so many of them that Dad calls them Los Conejos –the rabbits- and hides from them in his office: Mom's daughter Leticia calls me Burra like Abuelita and tries to make me like her –but I don't- just on basic principals; Damaris – ok we were puppies together but Julia, the Drama Queen, I bit her so the relationship there is somewhat strained; Indian Wells doesn't like the fact that upon occasion I use my teeth to make a point; and Sheradino calls me Perra Mala Mala because of the biting thing. On the other hand, I'm crazy about Pedro – maybe he can come over and play with me, snuggle and take me for long walks.

This whole leaving thing ... human betrayal is nothing new – history is full of it- so I just better get used to it, I thought as I made my way through the wac wac wac of my doggy door and remembered how Damaris and I had pioneered the doggy door together. Damaris is grown now – too big for the doggy door... kind of sad," I thought as I made my way to the fence – the fence that Dad made after reading <u>Siberian Huskies for Dummies</u>. This fence is designed to keep me in the yard, when I didn't want to leave and has just made the place look like a jail. Oh well, when under stress the best thing to do is to take a nap so I laid my head on the bottom rung of the fence and took a nap in the afternoon sun.

***

Indio, Saturday, March 6, 2010.

Oh, that was a great nap. Could have slept for a week. Maybe I did. Stretch ... oh stretch...all the way from my nose to the tip of my tail. Arch my back. Kick out my two back legs and shake all over. Feels great. Humans should try it; maybe they'd have fewer back issues. Now, I'll casually walk wac wac wac through the doggie door and back to the house to see if there's any food. I'm hungry. It was a long nap.

It looked that while I was sleeping the whole familia has shown up. Something is wrong. My Spanish has gotten pretty rusty since Dad and Mom have been talking in English almost exclusively but I recognize *perder* ... that's *lost* no big deal Dad is always lost when we're driving; Mom isn't much better, but *secuestrar* that means...Oh my Goodness ... that means kidnapped. I better check this out. I hope my Spanish is bad and not the news.

I overheard the following conversation:

"Stop crying Julia," Sheradino cautioned his four year old even though he was pretty close to it himself. No time for drama. We need to find them. Be strong. But Julia kept on crying and even her sister eight-year old Damaris' resolve was beginning to shake. Nobody was in very good shape.

"I was beginning to get worried when they didn't return as planned," Sheradino continued. "I waited almost a week, and then I called the airline – they hadn't shown up for their flight. With no news from the airline, I called the hotel* where they were staying and the staff confirmed that they had left on schedule. No word from Sinaloa. I haven't been able to reach anybody down there. And their rental car has not been returned.

"Then I got this note," Sheradino continued to read: "We have your parents held captive. If you want to see them alive again send 1$ million dollars in small bills. No Benjamins. Instructions to follow: Los Zetas."

"That's crazy," his half sister Leticia interrupted. Where on earth are they going to find a million dollars? He's a retired schoolteacher and she's a part timer at Costco. They don't have that kind of money – not even close."

"I know it doesn't make much sense, but I'm going to Sinaloa tonight. My Mom sacrificed for me – I can sacrifice

---

* *This was the same hotel where El Chapo (Shorty) Guzman was staying when the law recently -2014- caught up with him in the form of the American D.E.A. and the Mexican Marines.*

for her. I know my way around the area – I was just there last month. I'm strong as a bull; Los Zetas watch out."

"Now, Sheradino, you watch out," interrupted his wife Indian-Wells whose aristocratic looks and bearing belied a very humble Mexicali background. "We need you here. The girls and your new son Manuel need you ...your Padre La Familia. We all need you. Now go to the police. This is not Mexico ...maybe they're not Paisano – not your countrymen- but you can still trust them."

OK, I'll go talk to the police –I know officer Reymundo Ortiz down at the station – he's Paisano, but no border patrol-no migras please.

"Pedro, will you please calm down," Leticia told her first born. "And stop raising you hand ... this isn't school. Can't you tell we're having a very serious discussion?"

"Momi, the dog- Our Courage- is gone."

***

I must admit that I was a bit frightened when I began my quest, but when I looked back at my breed's history, I found that I was a proud descendent of a long and distinguished line of hero dogs. Now let me assure you that hero dogs are not exclusively German Shepherds or Collies or go by the name of Rin Tin Tin or Lassie.

Mine is a line of true hero dogs: the Siberian Huskies who carried the diphtheria vaccine that saved the lives of Alaska's Inuit children – Iditarod – The Serum run of 1924- as well as those Siberians who during World War II pulled the sleds through the snow that took wounded Russian soldiers from the front to the safety of forward aid stations. My breed has been celebrated in the literature of Jack London; the radio plays of Sergeant Preston and his lead dog King and most recently in the movie "Eight Below."

***

Well, that wasn't very hard. Just I just pushed the door open with my nose, out I went and I was on my way to Mexico. That latch never worked very well, anyway. The humans were so worried about Mom and Dad that nobody noticed the wac wac wac of the doggie door as I left or even the creaky gate when I pushed it open.

Maybe Indian Wells wouldn't let Sheradino try to rescue Mom and Dad but nobody is going to notice a dog –beautiful, willful and stubborn as I am – when I track down my humans –and save them.

Sheradino would get himself killed –he's brave, strong and smart –but no match for Los Zetas. I'm cautious and no threat unless of course you happen to be another female dog. Then I'll tear your lungs out – cautiously of course.

I followed a car out the gated complex and made my way west on Ave 48, South on Monroe and then West on Ave. 52. I planned to cross Route 86 - the main north south highway to and from the Mexican border and work my way along the Salton Sea outside the sight of humans, then to Westmorland, Brawley and follow Rt. 111 to Calexico and across to Mexicali.

Because of the heavy traffic at the downtown border crossing, I later changed my plans and went toward the small town of Holtville to cross at the east gate to Mexicali. I knew that I would need some help getting to the train – The

Beast- and on to Sinaloa- but humans and others have a way of showing up when you most need them. Then I'd sniff out Mom and Dad.

***

Now, back to my story. It was evening cool and the road to Route 86 was pretty easy. But then I said to myself:

Those tractor trailers were worse than the garbage trucks. They were noisy and their owners yelled at me if I got too close. They were dangerous as could be – I just looked at the bodies of some of my fellow coyotes – the canine variety. Now, I had to figure out how I was going to get over the road and not be road-kill myself?

Think girl! Then I just walked down the side of the road – not too close mind you – and looked for an opening.

Got it. That blue car stopped at the light – I caught them before it changed. I figured that I could hitch a ride or at least get across this darn road without getting killed. I used my charm and good looks:

It was an old blue Datsun. Humans were getting out – four of them – two adult humans – one female and one male; and a boy and a girl. The adults looked kind of angry:

"Look, my Serpents Teeth, if you kids don't stop fighting, I'm going to leave you by the side of the road and you'll starve to death or worse in this god-forsaken desert," the male adult, Joseph who was of average height and in his late 30s, said to the children.

"You can't do that," the boy, James, a nerd in training at about age 10, replied. "It would be tantamount to child neglect, abuse and besides that it's illegal.

Even I could tell that the adult human didn't mean it; the male human loved his kids to distraction and would die himself in this place for his kids if he had to.

"James hit me" Martha- the cute younger daughter- said and began to cry.

"You were in my sector of the back seat," her brother replied.

Mary, the adult female, cute as a button, blonde and significantly younger than her husband, could only smile to herself in relief that these monsters in training were her step kids and not her biological issue. But she loved them anyway – perhaps because she didn't have to.

Another reason to love them was because she had lost her only child Jessica not too long past. Would there be another baby? No. That one broke the mold. She died so early. Never really born.

"Look Father," Martha said – tears now a forgotten nuisance. "There's a beautiful wolf coming to us. Can I pet him?"

"Oh? Martha" James replied, "that's not a he –she's a she – we'll talk about that issue later- and not a wolf but what appears to be a Siberian husky."

"She's beautiful," Father agreed. But at this point, he thought to himself, I think I need to change my medication. Here I am in the middle of this God forsaken desert, with two bratty kids and my girlfriend.

And now there's a …Siberian husky sitting on my lap," Mary observed, "No, Martha, we can't keep her. Your father and I both work full time and, you know, dogs need a lot of attention – not like our cat."

"I'm hungry. I want to eat now," James demanded.

"...OK ..." Father replied. "There's a restaurant on the other side of the road – looks like something out of the 30s – we can get a hamburger and be on our way to Mexico with our blood sugar to a level where we might begin to resemble human beings."

In her most plaintive voice, Martha asked "Can we get a hamburger for the dog too. She's must be very hungry."

"OK, but then she's got to leave after that," Dad replied.

I waited patiently outside the restaurant until my newly found and somewhat querulous family emerged –with the promised hamburger -from the restaurant. Upon receipt of the hamburger – which I "wolfed" down- I left my new family and continued my journey to the banks of the Salton Sea and south to Mexico.

As I left, I thought about the family: Nice people, the three of them really want a dog –the male adult will be happy with one, the female adult will take in strays both human and canine, and the girl will love all animals and have a very tolerant husband. The boy is a cat person.

Nice people ...very nice people ... a lot of love between them, I thought again, but I saw a fault – as big and as deadly as the San Andreas that lies just east of here; a human fault that ran through that family and caused a deadly emotional earthquake in less for than five years; it broke them up and caused lasting personal devastation.

I just knew it. I know things. Maybe that's why Dad and Mom call me La Brujita – their little witch – but we dogs know things that humans can't see, hear or even feel.

Again, passing strange... Being with that family was like a visit from the late 70's –early 80's. Can't be. Or could it? Of course it can be. Dogs and humans know that time is mutable dimension and that seemingly unrelated events can intrude from what we term the past or future. Dogs live with that knowledge –humans deny this reality and could never deal with it even if they could understand it.

Too bad...nice people, if they only had a dog that relationship might make it, I thought and then trotted off to Desert Shores, the Salton Sea and a nice cool bath and a long cold drink.

***

The Salton Sea, California's largest lake, speaks to the geology and fickle course of the Colorado River that from time immemorial has defined the lives of the peoples living in the southwestern quarter of the United States and northwestern parts of Mexico. The lake now lies at the bottom of the Salton Sink over 200 feet below sea level and is the lowest, driest and hottest part of North America second only to Death Valley one mountain range to the east. 15 miles wide and 30 miles long, the Salton Sea is only a shadow of the mighty Lake Cahuilla, a vast inland sea that stretched from the Colorado Delta to the south and 100 miles north to what is now my home in Indio, California. Even now, the casual visitor can see about 200 feet above Route 86 something that looks like a giant bathtub ring. This easily observed "ring" defines the upper level of Lake Cahuilla; numerous seashells prove evidence of life of only 400 years past – a blink in geologic time.

As recently as the 16th century Spanish conquest, Lake Cahuilla was a food source for the native people who lived by the appearance and disappearance of their lake: If you look closely, you can see signs of their past fish traps. However, the original lake would soon disappear as the Colorado River completed its work of depositing the remains of what had once been a plateau, now the Grand Canyon, on its way to the sea. Effectively earthen dams, these deposits would close off Lake Cahuilla from its water source; nature then took its course and what water remained would soon evaporate.

Largely uninhabited desert until the early 20th century, the Salton Sink again filled with Colorado River water when an aqueduct, designed to transport water from the Colorado to the growing city of Los Angeles, malfunctioned and over he course of a little over a year effectively leaked a lake. Although expected to evaporate, the depression filled with water again – this time from agricultural runoff from recently irrigated farmland of Riverside and Imperial Counties that ran along its shores. This new "sea" also effectively covered a significant part of the Torres-Martinez Indian Reservation. An equitable arrangement for the loss of this land is still under negotiation.

Recreation followed the Salton Sea – not to be confused with Lake Cahuilla past or present. Sand sprouted a number of settlements- places like Desert Shores and Salton city that promised an easy, fun desert lifestyle. However by the late 50s, the lake had lost its desirability due to increasing saltification and pollution. What's left of their buildings and plans is now little more than the detritus of a failed dream. While the remaining white Americans still living there are but shades of half a century ago, the remnant numbers have been replaced by a poor but vibrant largely undocumented Mexican community that lives in fear of the Border Patrol – known as la Migra- and survives on meager wages paid by local white agriculture.

Pesticides from local agricultural irrigation runoff and toxic waste from the New River which drains from the 1 million plus inhabitants of Mexicali, Mexico, contributes to the witches brew of contaminates that now constitute its waters. Various schemes have been floated to deal with this fetid body of water but none has gained traction – much less funding. The possibility of just letting the lake evaporate would lead to toxic dust storms making life downwind virtually impossible. So it just gets worse: On hot dry 120 degree days when the wind is blowing the wrong way, the stench of dead fish and dying birds penetrates more than 20 miles from the lake – all the way north to Indio.

***

Approaching the Salton Sea, I trotted my way down toward the water's edge along what could be best described as Failure Avenue: To my right was an abandoned church and further down a shuttered food store. Even the boat dock didn't make it to the water that had evaporated down about six feet –nobody cared – nobody boated much less swam in the Salton Sea anymore.

My head was filled with memories: That tragic family from 30 years past which I had never known but treated me well, loneliness and not a little anger toward my family who had deserted me leaving me to survive in this God forsaken place - populated by some cactus, an occasional creosote bush, dead buildings, sandy gravel and hungry coyotes canine and otherwise.

Thirst prevailed over caution and I dove headfirst into the Salton Sea lapping up as much water as I could. And then I retched...and retched again...I even lost the hamburger the nice family had given me. The water was toxic and only my body's reaction saved my life. It felt like a week before I could shake the taste of salt and worse from my mouth or its stench from my body.

***

DESERT SHORES, EARLY SUNDAY MORNING, MARCH 7

Dog-tired and miserable I found a quiet safe place with my back to a rock. Ever the wolf, I slept fitfully through the night with one eye open until morning dawned through the cooling heavy mist off the Salton Sea.

Suddenly my open eye realized a fearful sight and my wolf reflexes jumped to respond: Less than 10 feet away I saw a giant –over 150 pound coyote -with blazing red eyes and long ivory teeth about to tear me apart.

No coward, I reflexed my body to a fighting position: Tail down, red eyes flashing, ears back, hair up on my back and baring my teeth...the teeth of a wolf calling on over a 100,000 years just longing for battle.

Bring it on," I snarled at the specter... "just bring it on ...I can tear the ear off a pit bull and scare the lights out of German Shepard twice my size...Just bring it on.

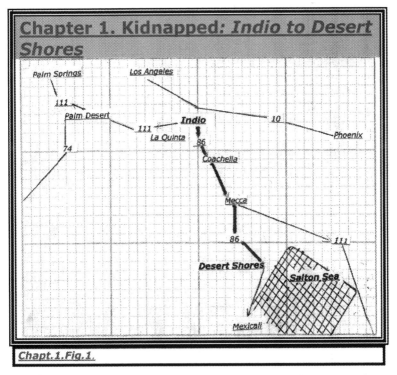

Chapter 1. Kidnapped: Indio to Desert Shores

Chapt.1.Fig.1.

Follow the attached the hand drawn map of my trip from Indio to Desert Shores: Leaving my house in Indio, I went to route 86 by way of Ave 48. Then I crossed #86 to get to Desert Shores where I spent a very sleepless night.

CHAPTER 2

FRIENDS INDEED

As I confronted that fierce coyote, I can assure you that I was one scared, tired and very angry dog:

"Just bring it on ...just bring it on," I snarled again at the specter.

But now, there was no longer a threatening fierce coyote, but an old fencepost. In its place, I heard: ... "temper... temper" which seemed to come from a cactus ... and "pride goes before a fall" from a rock then in a voice that appeared to come out of a creosote bush.

The Voice said: "OK. I know the story about the Pit Bull. Yes, you practically tore her ear off and then ran off to be comforted by your human. Your human was devastated to see you covered with blood until he found that it was the pit bull's blood and not yours. Poor pit bull got blamed and you got a tummy rub."

The best I could offer the creosote bush in my defense was to reply, "pit bulls are notorious bad gals and very ugly to boot so she had it coming."

"Anyway, how did you know that?" I asked.

"I'll cut you some slack on the pit bull," now a small mesquite tree returned my question and continued with a catalogue of my misdeeds, "but how about the poor old black lab? All he wanted to do was play ball with your male human and you practically tore his lungs out."

"Nobody plays with my human without my express permission which is rarely, if ever, granted. Are you familiar with the opera Tosca?" I returned.

"I hope whatever *IT-the Voice-* is doesn't know about the time Dad went to the mailbox without me," I thought. "When Dad came back, I could smell that puppy bitch on him so I just left the room jumped in their bed and peed."

So there I was in the middle of the desert, hungry, thirsty and very cranky arguing in succession with a cactus, a dried up old fence post, a rock, a creosote bush and a small mesquite tree, when, believe it or not who appeared to me, but:

***

"Officer Ariel Rabinowitz, United States Border Patrol, at you service." The voice was now a full size six foot plus border patrol officer, a migra, in full uniform who introduced himself to me as he emerged from the gloom of an early desert morning and stood as close as ten feet.

"What are you? First you're a coyote, then a dried up old fence post, a cactus, a rock, a creosote bush, a little mesquite and now a migra." I asked Officer Rabinowitz who was to be my new companion.

"And how do you know all that stuff about me? Are you some kind of angel?"

"You might say that I'm kind of an angel." Officer Rabinowitz replied. "I've been keeping an eye on you ever since you were a puppy."

"But now, Courage – yes, I know your name -let me tell you a little about myself," the good officer continued:"

"I'm what humans call a shape shifter. I'm named for Ariel, a shape shifter and Prospero's go for guy in <u>The Tempest</u>. Our sub species is called Jeden after the Czech word for *one*. Not the German word for *every* although there is a kind of relationship."

"For starters, we're called "One" because, unlike the grotesqueries of you mammals, we reproduce by asexual means – hence the name Jeden: We are born with a bud, which, like a fetus in mammals, gets first dibs on our energy and nutrition. Our life expectancy is about 200 years but at about 150 years our bud will supersede our needs and our bodies will serve primarily as a food source. I'm a tad over 100 and can already feel the needs of my bud sapping my energy."

"I guess you'd call me the ultimate single parent. My bud ...my buddy...get it? My buddy is always with me."

"I get it all right," I replied. "I heard it before. My Dad-"Popi" is always making puns and making Mom groan."

"Poor Popi...Poor Puzzled Popi...Poor Pooped Puzzled Popi..."

***

"You, Officer Rabinowitz, are indeed a cunning linguist, but besides puns and corny alliteration, why have I never met a shape shifter before?" I asked.

"Are you some freak of nature or has the desert gotten to me... and missing my humans ... worry in general...not to mention thirst and hunger," I continued.

"My type is not uncommon at all," the Jeden replied. "Many animals and plants change size and shape to hide or frighten their enemies. My appearance – that image you are talking to - is like a hologram and produced in a manner very similar to the luminescence that you see in various sea animals. The Googlers and other Silicon Valley types are working on the process but aren't even close."

"Just think about it," the Jeden continued. "Did you ever hear of a frog turning into a prince...or better yet, a man turning into a wolf? We shape shifters are a common subject of myth, legend and fairy tales. Vampires, who can turn into and out of bats, reproduce by sucking your blood and making you one of their own, perform incredible feats of physical strength, dexterity and speed, are the rage right now and have recently morphed into good and bad subspecies. The Greeks often found their gods turning from super natural to the just plain natural in order to assuage their lust: Zeus became a swan to force his affections on Leda; Daphne turned into a Laurel tree to thwart Apollo's desires. I most closely resemble the Pucas among the numerous creatures of fevered imaginations and mistaken identities. They are an Irish subspecies that can do you good or ill depending on how you treat them."

The Jeden went on "My favorite is the octopus. They change color and shape, swim, run and hide while maintaining the ability to squeeze through an opening two inches wide. Don't worry I'm not going to squirt ink at you."

I continued curious – curiosity is an issue with cats and not with dogs but I asked anyway: "Are you like a fairy or a goblin?

"No. Fairies, goblins, elves, Sasquatch, the wee people, Neanderthals and numerous other human sub species are now extinct do primarily to habitat destruction and outright genocide caused by Cro-Magans. Yes, the same species as your beloved humans and their not so beloved captors."

"Well," Officer Rabinowitz concluded, I'm getting tired and will soon go invisible. The Border Patrol Station is on the east side of #86, about a mile from here where the road goes from two lanes going north to one."

As I began the short walk to the Border Patrol Station, I happily wagged my tail at the prospect of food and drink and the good chance of renewed conversation with my new friend Officer Ariel Rabinowitz.

***

A word on the vagaries of La Frontera- American side: Border Patrol facilities are placed along major routes about 40 miles north of the border with Mexico. Travel south of the 40-mile limit from Mexico requires only a passport. However, to travel north of the 40-mile limit the Mexican visitor needs to obtain a visa stating reason for visit, destination and proof of Mexican financial security. This visa is good for three months at which time it must be renewed. It can only be granted at the border from an American official who verifies the *proffered information.*

The Border Patrol facility the Jeden and I visited is on route #86 and typical of most secondary checkpoints. You'll see three temporary buildings, replete with all the paraphernalia and antennas that seem to come with all government installations. There is a large covered area where the cars are stopped to review visitors and, if necessary, interdict illegal drug carriers and apprehend and return individuals without visas or the undocumented to their home country.

Officer Rabinowitz assured me that most migras are pretty nice, professional and that I should have little problem with them. He told me that, if I used my good looks and considerable charm, I should also be able to get some food and drink when I got there.

***

That morning just outside the Rt. 86 Border Patrol Station, Officer Georges Mount saw something most unusual.

"What is that?" the officer said to himself as he peered into the early morning mist from his post at the #86 Border Patrol station. "Is it a wolf? No, too small. A coyote. There's rumor of a giant coyote out in the desert. No, too pretty. It looks like a snow dog...like one of them Huskies I saw in "Eight Below." A husky in the desert, now that's weird."

"Come here boy, I'd like to pet you."

"Not so fast; I just don't like that guy," I said to myself. Then I gave him a fierce bite ...a real bone crusher.

"I'm gonna kill that dog," Officer Mount screamed in pain and drew his 38 service revolver.

"Not so fast," cautioned his superior, Captain Jose Gutierrez. "Our job is to interdict drug smugglers and apprehend and return undocumented immigrants to their home country. Not to kill stray animals."

I must admit. I really liked that guy Captain Gutierrez. I let him give me a lot of serious pets and, then he gave me a tummy rub – almost as good as the Dad tummy rub variety.

"Now, Officer Mount," Officer Gutierrez ordered, "please rewrite the report on the damaged government vehicle – it was the right fender not the left that you wrecked when you went careening out of here to apprehend that bratty white kid who may or may not have made an obscene gesture in your general direction.

As he grumped off in the general direction of the battered Border Patrol SUV, I heard Officer Mount say something to the effect that the white kid was driving a blue 1950 Packard with New York license plates. Passing strange, I met a family from the eighties, now a cop from the fifties and there are rumors of a witch from the future.

When my humans go to work it takes them forever to return home; when we play on the beach at Davenport, we're in the car and leaving in no time. I guess I'll leave it to over paid tenured human professors to ponder the mysteries of quantum mechanics. Doesn't make much sense to this poor ignorant dog.

***

From seeming out of nowhere, Officer Ariel Rabinowitz appeared to Captain Gutierrez and offered his services.

"Oh, I'm sorry, Officer Rabinowitz, I didn't notice you. I guess I was preoccupied with the behavior of my subordinate Officer Mount who wrecked a government vehicle while chasing the specter of some 50s kid in a blue Packard. We're a proud service, but even with our standards, sometimes we get a bad apple and, as a government entity, it takes forever to direct his path toward other employment."

"But I'm curious as to why you are here. What station do you work for?" Captain Gutierrez asked Officer Rabinowitz.

"Oh, I'm from the other side; sent here as a substitute" the Jeden replied.

"The other side? What other side?" Captain Gutierrez asked.

Oh, not THAT other side," the Jeden smiled back. "The other-side of the Salton Sea – the Border Patrol Station on #111. It's a long trip: You have to go either north to Mecca and then south on #86 or south on #111 Calipatria and north on #86. There's no ferry service across the Salton Sea."

"I agree, that's a long trip and I'm sorry that you were incorrectly notified that we needed a substitute. I've got two officers who were delayed because of an accident on #86 – an old Datsun rolled over – no serious injuries however – but my officers should be here soon."

While they were engaged in conversation, Officer Mount returned with a corrected report.

"Good job, Officer Mount," Captain Gutierrez encouraged. "Your shift is almost over and I just need to inquire – government regulations you know- how far along are you toward mastering Spanish, the Law Enforcement Program and the Physical Fitness requirement?"

"I don't know why I need to pass all them tests," Officer Mount grouched back at his supervisor. "I'm American and speak American – not Mexican. So why learn it. The Law Enforcement program at the College of the Desert is boring, the teacher doesn't know what she – just think a "she" cop-was talking about- and not relevant to my needs ... and the PE requirement, I earned this pot belly and intend to keep it."

Captain could only shake his head – it had been a long shift – and he just didn't have the energy or the patience to remind Officer Mount that the Mexican language was Spanish and his language was English and not American; the "Lady" Cop was a decorated veteran and head of a well know police department. The Physical Education test? He could only guess that Officer Mount had made the decision to eat bad and die fat.

"Just a small favor Officer Mount," could you stay just a little longer – our replacements are a little late," Captain Gutierrez asked.

***

"Unpaid overtime? Don't even think about it." Officer Mount replied." I'm going home. Just a minute – who are you? I don't recognize you. What's your name? Where are you from?"

"Let me introduce myself Officer Mount, I'm Officer Ariel Rabinowitz – evidently an unnecessary substitute for Patrol Officers who have been detained on official business.

"Are you Jewish? Officer Mount asked and offered that he graduated from George W. Hewlett High School in Long Island near New York City. "I graduated with a degree in Practical Arts. There are a lot of Jews there. Real smart. A lot of them had names like Rabinowitz... a lot of witzes and bergs. I remember an Ivan Rabinowitz –never sure if he was real or just made up by some wise guy."

Captain Gutierrez had to bite his tongue and not remind Officer Mount that you earned a diploma – not a degree from high school. However he did have to remind Officer Mount that questions of religion were forbidden much as the rest of the litany of no-nos inclusive of but not exclusive of age, national origin, race, sexual orientation and marital status.

Not a minute past the end of his shift, Officer Mount stalked way from the Border Patrol Station and got into his car, an 8 cylinder Camaro, glass packs noisier than a garbage truck – chopped, channeled and lowered in the rear – I guess Officer Mount hadn't taken auto mechanics – with the radio tuned up high to Rush Limbaugh's latest rant contra leftist political correctness and other liberal ghosts, goblins and things that go bump in the night. Home to his trailer a TV blaring Fox news, his favorite easy chair and the first crack to open of a six pack of Bud Light.

My new friend Captain Gutierrez shrugged his shoulders – sighed about his issues with Officer Mount -and related to Officer Rabinowitz some rumors of a giant, fierce coyote that had everything in the desert with four legs scared to death. "You had better watch out for that beautiful Siberian," he cautioned.

In light of that conversation, I looked up at the Jeden and asked with my eyes if that "fierce coyote" had been one of his illuminations; he signaled back that is was not. "Que pasa?" I thought.

"Well, I had better get going it's a long walk to Calipatria and the bus home," Officer Rabinowitz said to Captain Gutierrez.

"Wait a minute," Captain Gutierrez offered. "My replacement should be here shortly and I'll give you a lift.

I'm going in that direction myself. There's rumors of a big movement of undocumented under the direction of Mario Felix – super Coyote- headed up this way and I need to do some investigation."

"No thanks," Officer Rabinowitz replied, "I always make it a point to take public transportation."

I could only think that I would prefer a ride in a nice cool police car to a long walk in a hot dry desert, but evidently Jedens always take public transportation. My Jeden was obviously tiring and his luminescence was increasingly rough around the edges; even his voice was sounding old and tired.

In less than a mile, my Jeden went invisible. I could tell that Officer Rabinowitz was having trouble keeping up with me so I'd dog trot ahead and wait for the good Jeden to catch up. From time to time, I was able to find a little shade and some water from a small irrigation ditch, but believe me; by the time we got to Calipatria I was one tired, hot and thirsty puppy.

Although it had been a while since I had seen my Jeden or we had talked, I could feel that the presence was near me. When the bus finally came, I could sense something like a small disturbance in the atmosphere when the bus driver opened the door, looked around, looked around again and closed the door. He felt it too.

It was still the heat of the day...but I was able to find some shade and some water that the kind people at the Seven Eleven had left out for hot dry pets to drink. I needed to get some much-needed shut-eye – dogs sleep a lot. In fact, when Mom and I first lived together, she thought I was sick because I slept so much – "not sick, Mom –just a dog." I told her – I think she understood – but humans are very bad at "dog" while dogs are very good at "human."

***

As I waited for the Sand Dog, I remembered my friends canine and human from the Bay Area: My Mom and Dad, Uncle Al, that nice John from church (must be friendlier to him next time we meet) and all the people who called me Beautiful Dog when I took my walks with Dad.

I could never forget that handsome Pointer I met while cavorting on the beach outside of Davenport. – I never did get his name. He was cute, but all he wanted to do was work; all I wanted to do was play. We'd run, I'd punch, and sniff and then he'd start to dig. We'd run; then he'd dig. Must have been a Googler or some engineering type. Face it, I may come from a long line of working dogs, but I'm 100% party animal.

And Breta. Talk about looks – pure white husky-German shepherd mix. Gorgeous blue eyes. We'd party for a while but then he seemed to be more interested in my human than in me. I'm a proud dog-not some kind of imitation human. I love my special humans –after all I'm risking my life, Purina dog food and cool morning walks to save them from some really bad other humans – but really, when it comes to party time, I put on the dog.

But as I slept, I forgot the others and dreamed of my true forever love:

***

Coachella, Monday Morning, March 8, 2010

The day after Courage met Officer Ariel Rabinowitz, Sheradino De Leon grumbled his way to visit Town of Coachella Police Chief, Reymundo Ortiz, his old friend, paisana (countryman) and fellow group member. The two even looked like brothers. Like Sheradino, the chief was a solid hunk of a man short of statue but broad of shoulders and deep of chest who just couldn't lose the ferocity of his Mexican mustache and a smile that belied the seriousness of police work.

"Hola Sheradino, que pasa?" His old friend Chief Ortiz greeted him on arriving in his office and asked: "To what do I owe the honor?'

"Here have some coffee. It's Starbucks – straight from the first Starbucks in Coachella- a welcome sign of civilization in the East Valley. "

"But, wait a minute, you look awful," his friend observed. "You haven't started drinking again? Have you? You weren't at group last night."

"Not that," Sheradino replied. "Much worse."

"Something wrong with the family? Are your girls – Indian Wells, Julia and Damaris –and your son and heir Manuel- OK? Something at work?"

Without saying a word, Sheradino handed the ransom note to his old friend.

The Police Chief read:" We have your mother and her husband captive. If you want to see them again alive, we will need to have one million dollars in small bills – no Benjamins. Instructions to follow: Los Zetas."

"I don't even know what a "Benjamin" is," Sheradino replied.

"That one is easy," the Chief answered. "Benjamin refers to the United States $100 bill which has a picture of Benjamin Franklin on the front. That denomination is the currency of the drug trade. The kidnapper fears, with some justification, that if you used a "Benjamin" it might be easily traced by serial number. It also shows that the kidnapper – or one of them anyway- is an American and plans to use the ransom money in the United States. Any other country wouldn't trace it.

"I appreciate your concern and questions. Worry, anger, guilt and a sleepless night are part of the ransom." The Chief observed.

"As you know, Sheradino, you learned in Citizenship Class that kidnapping is a federal offence and an FBI matter, and, in your case, there will be an obvious international aspect to this case. I will only be peripherally involved."

"But I do have a few questions and some observations: First, where did your Mom and her husband get the money? Did they win the Lotto or something?"

"Not that I know of," Sheradino responded. "Believe me, if Mom won the Lotto, I'd be the first to know. She's always talking about what she'd do if she won it – her latest thing is buying houses. She says that when she wins, she's going to buy everyone in the family a house. It's her fantasy and even her husband indulges her in it. She remains a part timer at Costco and a Mexican cleaning lady; he's a retired school teacher with no outside income."

***

"Oh, excuse me Sheradino for the interruption, but your nephew Pedro just reported a missing dog – a beautiful Siberian Husky- to Idalia Gonzalez, our Animal Control Officer and unofficial Doggie Migra. It's dangerous for a stray dog in the desert – natural predators like coyotes, unnatural ones like humans who can torture and kill untended pets, plus your basic car and truck killings and the rigors of heat and lack of water. Is there anything you want us to do?"

"Courage can take care of herself," Sheradino replied. "She's tough as nails, beautiful, manipulative and she bites. She's the last thing in the world I need to worry about at this time."

"OK, now back to our review: How long have they been missing and when did you last know of their whereabouts?"

"They were planning first fly to Mazatlan and then rent a car and go to Sinaloa to visit relatives just outside Culiacan. They checked out of the hotel as planned and rented the car – it was after that that I lost track of them. I tried to contact our relatives but with no luck. It' been about a week since I lost them," Sheradino responded.

"Now about the note," Officer Raymundo Ortiz continued. "It's very odd that there is no time or place noted for the transfer. I'm not an authority, but I doubt very much that the Los Zetas would bother with a Mexican cleaning lady and an old white schoolteacher. Whoever it is, is probably trying to intimidate by using that dread name and is an obvious amateur at this kind of thing."

"I will be forwarding the note and the envelope with my observations to the FBI. They have far more sophisticated forensic capabilities than we have out here in the desert. We don't have the authority, technology, and training or time to adequately address your case. I'm sure the FBI will be in touch with you soon."

"And in closing Amigo don't even think about playing Zorro and rescuing Mom and Dad. There's an obvious American connection here -just as dangerous as anything in Mexico -that could be living just as close to you and your family as your next door neighbor."

"Try and be cool. Welcome to a little bit of hell. And remember, that you have a friend in the Coachella Police Department." Officer Ortiz concluded.

Sheradino returned home to await a call from the FBI.

***

A little bit later the morning of Sheradino's visit to the Coachella Police Station– actually a lot later because bad people sleep late - Caleb was boasting of his latest criminal exploit to his most incredulous and abusive Moma Sycorax. They angrily shared a modest apartment in the neighboring town of La Quinta.

Caleb bragged to his mother: "I did everything right: I used the computer in the library when I wrote the note – no trace – and put on latex gloves when I handled the material – no fingerprints – sealed the envelope and dropped it in La Familia De Leon's mail box.

"You are as dumb as you're ugly," his mother shot back at him and gave him a pinch that practically tore the right side of his face off and left a terrible bruise. "I suppose you licked the envelope shut – leaving your accursed DNA for the FBI to analyze. Yes, the FBI, Dumb Head, because, Rocks for Brains, if you hadn't been kicked out of school for bad behavior and excessive dumbness, you would have learned that kidnapping is a federal capital crime."

"And the note," she said with a face contorted with anger and breath hot with saliva and garlic, "lets discuss the note:"

"What, no time, place or method to make the exchange? What are they supposed to do – go to Mexicali and wave around one million dollars in small bills when they're imprisoned somewhere south of Culiacan?"

"But my favorite part, Idiot Child, is the thing about Los Zetas. They are not very nice people and have tortured and killed any number of narco thugs and innocents whom they perceived as competitors or just plain bothersome. Not that I would mind, but are you interested in having your deformed body left somewhere in the desert outside of Nuevo Laredo and your empty head dropped unceremoniously off a bridge in Tijuana?"

More from exhaustion than bile, Sycorax briefly dropped her tirade to listen to Caleb make some excuses for his repeated lapses of judgment.

"Nobody's perfect, Moma. I just thought that Los Zetas would intimidate them, and, yes I forgot the part about DNA and a date and place for the ransom. Do people really negotiate this kind of thing?"

"Do people really negotiate thing kind of thing," Caleb says, Sycorax thought as she entered into a one-hag pity party. Life isn't fair. I was lonely … desperate is more like it. I think his Dad was from someplace near Russia …pretty gamey smell to him…ugly as sin…and stupid –that guy could really do stupid."

***

"Same old story," Sycorax continued to herself. "One tequila, two tequila, three tequila floor. And floor is where Caleb happened. When I woke up I saw Mr. Coyote Ugly and flew out of there. Couldn't get rid of it – Santorum was president at the time – so I was stuck with Caleb. Every time I look at him I think of the inherent treachery of tequila."

"There were others," she reminded herself: "Priscilla's father - That man - devilishly handsome, tall, dark Spaniard. Boy did I love him. And Antonio, I wonder if Priscilla knows about that – well, I trained him well for my daughter's pleasure. Dark, built like a cat and oh so energetic. I was his first woman. I guess you could call me a cougar. I agree with my feline namesake. There's nothing like fresh meat."

"I was a virgin once myself," she remembered. "But I fixed that problem as soon as possible with my handsome cousin George. I was lucky 13 and he was in his twenties. It was my idea, but he was pretty easy to persuade. He bought it in Viet Nam, so I heard, but by that time I was on to other things and other men."

"Wouldn't it be nice to blame my parents for my behaviors – criminal and otherwise, but it just won't work," she thought. "They were both hardworking and well educated. They never missed one of my baby brother's football games. We could have been the Eldridge Clever Family – and I a female version of Beaver – or was that beaver."

"College?" she thought, "it was a haze of drugs, booze and men – even a few women. I worked my way through that fraternity –Alpha something – man by man."

"I paid for all that action with an abortion and those nasty warty things that I just can't get rid of. Big deal. I was rewarded for my fun times with a bachelors degree – or better yet a degree in bachelors although there were a few married men thrown in the mix."

"In most cases, a Liberal Arts Bachelor leads to burger flipping. Me too. So I did my time working in a local burger joint dressed in that awful uniform and bringing home little money and a big deep fry stink. Selling drugs and organizing the cross the border business was a natural – I spoke fluent Spanish and had already experienced the consumer end of the trade."

"I was a pussycat back then or maybe just a pussy, but now I'm a cougar" she told herself. "Not the prettiest thing in world – terrible acne and unquenchable body odor- but I persuaded myself that I was beautiful and convinced a few others along the way that indeed I was.

A girl has to take initiative and define her world, it ain't pretty, but it's the way life is," she concluded.

***

Somewhat refreshed from her one hag pity party, Sycorax continued the inquisition of her unwanted son: "Now, Dummy, where do you think those two –a retired teacher and Mexican cleaning Lady –would put their hands on one million dollars?"

"Cut me some slack on that one Moma," Caleb retorted while braced for a pinch, a cramp or a simultaneous punishment:

"I hear things. And I heard that the old lady had just won the lotto. $1,000,000. Now, remember when I found out that Jose had just withdrawn $2,000 from the bank and had it with him in his apartment. All I had to do was cut the screen to their bedroom, put a gun to his head —scare the daylights out of Suzie – and collect the $2,000."

"You were happy with me then, and took your part of the loot and bought a new pair of shoes and a case of tequila."

"I guess you've got good ears but you're dumb as a box of rocks, seriously ugly and kind of dangerous to have around so I'm going to send you Mexico to work for your Tio (Uncle) Antonio. You should be able to arrange the ransom and get to know a little of the family business. If you mess up, Tio Antonio will warm you up with torture, medieval style, and then blow your brains out.

"I'll fly down later in my Big Black Town car"

"Witch," Caleb said to himself. "I hate that old hag. I hope she crashes and..."

"I heard that," Sycorax shot back and laid a cramp on Caleb so severe that he almost lost his lunch.

Chapter 2. Friends Indeed: *Desert Shores to Calipatria*

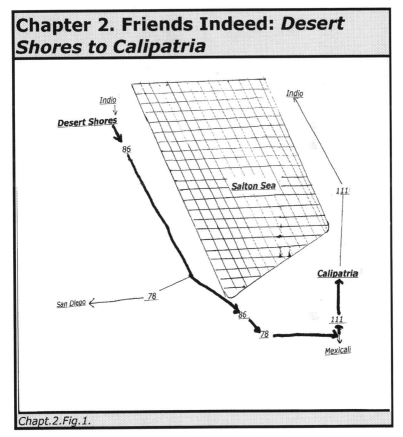

Chapt.2.Fig.1.

After I got over the pleasure of meeting the Jeden in the person of Officer Ariel Rabinowitz, we walked together from Desert Shores to the Border Patrol Station on Route #86 in Salton City. I said good-by to the Jeden in Calipatria and got some well earned sleep at that town's 7-11

CHAPTER 3

HERMANOS: MALE AND FEMALE

CALIPATRIA, MONDAY, MARCH 8.

Dog tired from a long day of adventure, I slept the night behind the Calipatria 7-11, and as I slept, I dreamed of home and woke up to:

"Tuma! Tuma!

"Is it really you? My love ... you beautiful powerful animal... You are the dog...Let me smell you – oh wow – give you a few love hits ... Oh Tuma you've come all the way to this awful desert to marry me ... we'll have beautiful puppies ...two alphas... running together... leading the pack..."

Tuma was really there. I had awakened to his gorgeous presence...his wonderful smell. He was really there – in Calipatria in the middle of the desert.

"Courage, calm down," Tuma said as I danced around shaking my booty in eager anticipation of the mating of the century perhaps of the last 15,000 years when our ancestors first joined forces with humans.

Come on Tuma, you big lug," I replied. "Come on, let's have fun. It's party time. Don't be so serious."

"Courage, you can't – remember you had the operation – no mating and no puppies – and I won't – I'm that way."

"Oh Tuma, there's got to be some way around the operation – never stops humans from mating – and yes, I know you're that way but you can be cured. There must be a Michel Bachman for dogs – straighten you out."

"I'm not sick; I don't want to be cured; I don't want to be straightened out. Keep those prejudiced humans out of my orientation. And don't forget, you're a dog and no mating without estrus. So just calm down, Coyote Ears."

"Coyote Ears," I snarled at my platonic friend. "Those *Coyote Ears*, my dear friend are somewhat large for my breed but accentuate my fine facial features. I'm pure Siberian husky although there has been some talk about my lack of papers. Not withstanding some pettiness about documentation, I am proclaimed by 'one and all as "Beautiful Dog...

Then it slipped out. I called him "Joto." (Spanish for Gay –not complimentary)"

"Joto? So now I'm Joto. You Bitch," Tuma growled back. "Besides that, the Joto business is so politically incorrect that, if you weren't a little female, I could just bite you."

I'm Joto and proud of it," the big dog continued. "You Butch-Bitch. I've seen you pee – you try to pee like a guy. And you can't. So there."

"And Butch-Bitch isn't just as politically incorrect as Joto?" I barked back. "What you interpreted as *trying to pee like a guy* was when I was just claiming me territory. Sometimes squatting is very inconvenient; it just doesn't do the job."

At this point, after all the barking and snarling, we both groaned and realized that we were the best of friends – and friendship was a more profound and powerful relationship than mere lovers. But I must admit not half as much fun.

I found out later, Tuma had already saved my life once and would again numerous times. Our mission – while maybe not leading a pack and having puppies – was a difficult and dangerous one. Friendship was not only a beautiful relationship but also necessary for our survival.

***

Tuma, what are you doing? Scratch...scratch ...I know all us dogs scratch but you are constantly scratching...why are you doing that?

"Fleas," he replied.

Fleas, like on a dirty dog? Mom is always trying to put flea medicine on me, but I don't let her. I move quickly – sometimes I even give kind of a caution bite – not hard – but to say back off lady. Dad just watches.

"Fleas, it's part of the lifestyle," he replied. "No, before you ask ... well, yes, there were a few encounters with other dogs so inclined along my trip down here and some of them probably had fleas ...but it's really the life style ...the life style you and I will be leading until we complete our mission."

"We're road warriors now, Courage. Hunger, thirst, cars-trucks and yes fleas...it's all part of the journey," he concluded.

Oh Tuma, I was so excited by your appearance- then by my obvious disappointment that ours was to be a Platonic relationship – and then the distraction of the flea business - that I forgot to ask, "why are you here."

***

"It's a long story, but I'll try to keep it short" my friend Tuma replied: "You'll remember when my fathers and I left Sunnyvale to live in the forest above Santa Cruz. You went back to the desert shortly thereafter."

"I remember it well, when I returned. I was heartbroken," I said.

"I loved it there. Cool forest. Animals to chase..." Tuma continued. "But then business interests sent one of my fathers to Denver and the other to Seattle. In the confusion, I got left. The new owners of our house kicked me out, and I narrowly escaped Animal Control and certain death in the shelter where only the cute survive."

"Oh, Tuma if I had only known. My humans and I could have done something. While you were suffering, I was choosing my favorite dog food. I feel so inadequate." My commiseration was heartfelt.

"There I was in the middle of the woods, hungry and lonely and terrified by the sudden appearance of a giant ferocious mountain lion – I figured, Tuma give it your all, and..."

I know Tuma ...I know ...it was Officer Ariel Rabinowitz...

"Of the department of Fish and Game," Tuma replied.

"When I met him the Jeden was a terrifying coyote... then a rock...then a cactus...then Border Patrol ..." I told my friend.

Officer Rabinowitz informed me that I should head south and meet up with you in the desert." I said to him: "Desert?

Are you crazy? I'm built for 20 below – not 120 above. Get a Mexican Hairless to do the job."

Then the Jeden said, "Courage needs you. And I melted like butter in the hot sun. It was to be a difficult and dangerous journey: Crossing #17 by Santa Cruz was the easy part. Then I worked my way south and east past Hollister and down the interior mountains. I crossed #101 near Bakersfield and crossed #5 just north of LA and went through Lancaster. I was able to cross #10 at Indio and, like you made it down #86 and east to the Salton Sea."

"I don't know how I survived. I saw a lot of dead brother and sister dogs …cats…coyotes …raccoons and various other animals too disfigured to recognize. Somehow I just knew when to make my move across the road and when not to… those insights could have been the Jeden informing me, but after our initial meeting he went invisible."

"I got here a day before you did," Tuma concluded.

"Were you the coyote they were all talking about or was it the Jeden," I asked.

"It was not me," he replied. "I outweigh the largest male coyote by a good 50 pounds. Coyotes, while I don't like them and they are exceeding ugly, are very clever and have thrived in the human environment unlike our ancestors the Gray Wolf.

"There are coyotes all over the desert," Tuma continued. They work in pairs: A large male coyote – and we all know how you respond to large male canines – would invite you for dinner with the family - and you would accept the invitation. He, his female mate and the pups, would then make you the main course."

"You didn't know it at the time, but there was a large male coyote following you. I am assured that his intentions were far from honorable. It was not a pretty sight. But I took care of business. His mate is now a widow; his pups are orphans. They are all candidates for predation – probably by other coyotes."

"Oh, Tuma, you saved me. You are my hero."

***

But before we continue with my the story of my quest just a few notes about us dogs:

Over 15,000 years ago a few Gray Wolves decided to join human settlements someplace in the cold reaches of Far East Asia. These wolves, my great grandparents, became the Huskies, Malamutes and other members of the Spitz family of dogs. They were the pioneers who pulled the sleds that moved humans and their belongings across the land bridge from Asia to North America to settle two continents. My family of Siberians, fast forty-pound durable light eaters, also proved indispensible to the exploration of the earth's polar regions. We were the first dogs to see the north and south poles. Our humans couldn't have done it without us.

Similar to our wolf pack heritage, we work in eight to twelve dog sled teams often led by an alpha male and female. We remain Apex predators: Given the chance and in the company of a colleague or two we can take down the young and weak among domesticated livestock although we often settle for lesser fare.

Our hearing greatly exceeds that of humans in the high range and my flexible ears enable me to accurately locate the source of the sound; my sense of smell is 100,000 to one million times more powerful than my human friends and my wet nose directs the perception to my olfactory lobe. Although humans may surpass us in daytime vision and I envy their height advantage, we best our friends in night vision and sense of movement.

I also make a great pet – that is if you can deal with my energy, independence and good looks. You may ask, "Then why, with all your talents, do you dogs -particularly you Huskies- consort with humans- an obviously lower order species?

Easy: We've been looking after you for 15,000 years. What other species has the patience?"

Cats? ...Yeah, right.

***

Coachella, Wednesday Morning, March 10.

While Tuma and I were still reacquainting and planning our next move, Sheradino was meeting with FBI Special Agent, Malcolm MacDuff.

At his home in Coachella, Sheradino cautiously answered the door to welcome Malcolm MacDuff, Special Agent, F.B.I.. After checking out his ID, Sheradino offered Agent MacDuff a cup of Starbucks coffee and began to tell his side of the case. They talked alone: Indian Wells was at work; Damaris and Julia were at school and baby boy Manuel was with his aunt Leticia in Indio.

"I'm sorry for checking you out, but with Mom's kidnapping and Chief Ortiz at the local Coachella Police Station warning me about strangers, I just figured I couldn't be too careful," Sheradino said.

"I'm especially nervous when my family is here – in fact, I was just planning to go down to Wal-Mart to buy a gun to defend them. In Mexico, you can get in real trouble if you have a weapon, but in the United States it seems as if they want you to have the best money can buy," he said.

"I can't offer any advice about owning a weapon, Agent MacDuff replied. "The FBI is charged with defending the constitution and the courts have determined that the second amendment states that your right to have a firearm is not to be infringed – however, I caution you that those things are often more dangerous to the owner and his family than to the perpetrator – so just be careful."

Please forgive me," Agent MacDuff continued: "Here, we are debating the constitution and I haven't formerly introduced myself. I will be the Special Agent in charge of your case in line with the FBI's stated mission to combat transnational/national criminal organizations and enterprises. With the possibility of Los Zetas involvement- although we all doubt the veracity of that claim- your case will be receiving special attention and cooperation with the Mexican government."

"Just a few minutes, Sheradino, to review your file," agent MacDuff advised: "It says here that you were born in Mexico to Francisca Sarabia who raised you as a single parent until she married your step father and moved to the United States. I can't help but notice that your Mom sacrificed a lot for you."

"Moving to the United States with your parents in the mid-nineties," he continued, "you got into some trouble – nothing serious – in fact the only evidence of your bad choices is a tattoo of your mother's name on your chest. You developed an alcohol problem, but you've been clean and sober for over 10 years and remain an active member of your group."

"Sheradino, you're a model citizen: Naturalized, making progress in English, hard worker – devoted family man – to your immediate family in Coachella and your extended family in Mexicali and Sinaloa. Do you want to know anymore," he concluded.

"No, that's enough. I think you know more about me than I know, Agent MacDuff," Sheradino replied.

"It's part of the job," said Agent MacDuff, but can we continue this conversation in Spanish?"

"Sure," Sheradino replied, "but do you speak Spanish? You're tall, white, red haired, blue-eyed –your name isn't even Spanish."

***

The following conversation is translated from the original Spanish.

"Beware of stereotypes," Agent MacDuff replied. "I was always interested in foreign languages. In high school I studied Latin and later Spanish. In college at Brigham Young, I majored in Spanish language, Hispanic literature and history. My minor was economics. I planned to pursue a career in international business."

"However, as a member of the Church of Jesus Christ of the Later Day Saints, a Mormon, I was obligated to perform two years missionary service – my choice, and an obvious one, was Mexico. I lucked out of military service due to a low draft number," he continued.

"By the time I had completed my service, I was at a loss – business no longer held an appeal for me– but I wasn't sure what I wanted to do. The last thing in the world I contemplated was law enforcement or the FBI – the Eliot Ness thing turned me off. But I needed work and the FBI had a position for a linguist: From that it was a move to Special Agent and then the Hostage Rescue Team."

"Like you, I have two girls and a young son. Both girls are in college, the boy is a senior in high school, and I have aged parents. I hate to think of what you and your family are going through right now," he concluded.

"Now that we've introduced ourselves, have you heard anything about the situation of your mother and her husband?"

"Yes Agent MacDuff," Sheradino replied. "I just got a call from Tio Memo who was visiting his kids in Arizona. And he had just received a call from Delfinia who went to visit my Tio Simon and his wife only to find them inside their house, terrified to open the door and just about out of food from the little bodega they run next door. As the thugs took away Mom and Dad, they threatened my Tio's life if they called the authorities. He heard the thugs say something about taking them to a ranch just outside of El Dorado."

"That squares with our information," Agent MacDuff replied. "We checked out your relatives in Sinaloa and found them to be innocent of any involvement."

"We also reviewed your recent and numerous visits to Mexico to see if there was any involvement on your part. You're clean."

"Me, you checked out me to see if I was part of a plot to kidnap my own mother," Sheradino exclaimed.

"Everyone a suspect until proven otherwise," Agent MacDuff replied. "Just doing our job – in matters of this kind – no stone goes unturned. You'll be interested to know that our lab has just returned their analysis of the envelope and note that Chief Ortiz sent to us. We always try to work with local law enforcement –and your chief is first rate."

"The US end of the operation appears to be a small time –Narco Thug wanna be who goes by the name of Caleb. He's a person of interest by local authorities for a number of mostly minor crimes in the area, but appears to have gone big time when he is alleged to have robbed your brother at gunpoint. He took off for Mexico a few days ago."

"Like so many kids who failed at school and were too cool to avail themselves of programs like Job or Conservation Corps, Caleb just felt he had to be a Wise Guy. Background: Absentee father, abusive mother – not the sharpest knife in the drawer but bright enough to pass the California Exit Exam and if he applied himself – a reasonably good life. Well there's always hope."

"Just one more thing, Sheradino: Before I go to Mexico to check out this situation on the ground, I have a question about a dog –a beautiful Siberian Husky who appears to have teamed up with a fearsome Malamute. I understand that the dog in question belongs to your Mom and her husband. As I understand it, these dogs are heading to Mexico and have successfully avoided cars, trucks, outraged cat owners, garbage collectors and well-armed farmers. Do you know anything about this," Agent MacDuff concluded.

That can only be Courage, she's a true hero dog" Sheradino replied.

"Now back to English – my first language," Agent MacDuff concluded.

***

Brawley Area, Monday, March 8 through March 15.

"I love it…. I just love it," I heard myself barking. "Tuma and I are having so much fun – acting like two coyotes as we made our way past Westmorland and south to Brawley."

I love everything about it: The hunting, the teaming with Tuma to see who will bluff and who will strike, the fear in my victim, tearing apart, our prey and wolfing him down. Wagging my tail the whole time – I am truly Nos Lobita, a worthy heir of the Gray Wolf pack- the most feared killing machine of all time."

"Even eluding the owners of pussycats, small rabbits and yes, yappy little dogs was great fun. They'd get real close… very angry …and then we'd run away."

"Cats are my favorite with chickens a close second…never had a chance to take down anything larger…"

"Now my human friends, lest you think your pooch a homicidal monster, look to yourself. If we didn't do what we do, nature would be out of balance and even you humans would have issues. Your herds of cattle, sheep, and goats – and even in some societies, dogs, flocks of chickens and ducks are raised and killed for their meat. They never had a chance. All of our victims did."

"And your hunters use human technology to kill the biggest and the strongest of their prey. We benefit the totality of our victims by killing the young, the old and the weak. The remnants strengthen the species."

"And yes, Tuma and I are opportunistic diners: While I have a hatred of vegetables- equaled only by five year old human males – I'm not adverse to a tasty morsel of road kill or some particularly succulent garbage."

"But, it's not all fun and games. The desert is hot and dry – water is only available from irrigation ditches. And I miss my humans dreadfully – the walks with Dad and the naps on the air conditioning duct in our Indio home. These memories are enough to make me whine."

"Plus I hate these darn fleas. Scratch...scratch...all daylong, all night long and under the most embarrassing circumstance – I'm Beautiful Dog –not Dirty Dog. Aren't I? "

***

On our way to the border we passed through Brawley – which boasted the most succulent garbage of the whole trip so far.

Now a *bit about Brawley, which is a sad agricultural town of 25,000 souls. Unlike the Salton Sea Cities just to the north which are failed attempts at pleasure seeking fun in the sun, Brawley was planned with parks and a library and central city buildings designed for the desert heat. The lower level overhangs shield the shopper from the broiling desert sun while the upper stories of these buildings offer apartments for those living there.*

It never worked. Even the town's founder - a land developer whose name was Braley- refused to have the town named after himself hence the spelling Brawley. The town can only claim the lowest of the good – like income and educational attainment- and the highest of the bad such as unemployment and crime. The detritus of late 20th century car culture – fast food, car repair, surrounds the central part of the town. The population is over 80% Latino

After passing through Brawley and enjoying a large sampling of that municipalities' garbage, we decided to leave the noise, danger and dust of Route 111 and headed east on Route 78 and then south to Holtville crossing Route 8. Then we took Route 533 through the farms and hamlets along the way to the eastern and most recently built Border Crossing with Mexicali. This way we could avoid the traffic through Calexico and the hassle of the Central City Border Crossing some twenty miles to the west.

***

Ever since I left the Salton City Route 86 Border Patrol Station, I kept hearing the word coyote – not of the canine kind like Tuma dispatched – but a human coyote…some kind of werewolf perhaps. Believe me, after meeting up with Jeden just about anything was possible.

Well, that kind of coyote – the Mario Felix kind that Officer Gutierrez talked about– are indeed human and – like most humans – some are bad and some are good and most are just doing their job whether legal or illegal. For a price, the Coyote promises the immigrant to get him, her or they across the border from Mexico to the United States. When finally in the United States, they get them in contact with friends, family and potential employers.

With the population of the desert and desert cities largely Latino and conversant in Spanish, I couldn't really tell who was documented and who was not documented nor did I really care –that's the job of I.C.E.

The undocumented can jump the border in any number of ways: They can cross the lightly guarded desert border in Arizona, present forged documents, swim across the Rio Grande– hence the pejorative name "wetbacks," climb the border fence now often doubled, cross at a border check point and run like mad, boat around the deep water fence in Tijuana or tunnel just about anywhere– the preferred method of drug traffickers.

Dad tells of an extreme example when one of his students, after failing to jump the border two times, swam the New River – the most polluted river in North America and a conduit for toxic waste from Mexicali to the Salton Sea – and was caught by Officer Mount. The student had such a foul odor that the migra just let him past. Or so the story goes.

The border between Mexico and the United States sees hundreds of thousands of legal transients every day - most of whom travel by car but also by bus or on foot or even by plane. They cross for strictly legal reasons either for work, shopping, tourism or visiting friends and relations. The passport and visa requirement has only slowed the lines of dangerously over heated cars patiently waiting to enter El Norte.

It's a lot easier to go south than to go north. Human trafficking has produced some of our country's best workers – those people who tend your garden, mind your children and clean your houses. Mom crossed the border legally to harvest the crops and stayed: Her first job was in a laundry, then cleaning houses and on to retail work with Costco. She learned English at College of the Desert in their adult education program and gained her citizenship.

She did it the right way; others haven't. The multi-billion dollar drug trade is hard to resist for any enterprising young man: No educational requirements, it's easy to learn, hormone driven and romantic – there are actually songs written and performed to glorify the exploits of particularly successful narco-traficantes.

The drugs go north to feed the American insatiable desire for cocaine and meth; the money and guns go south to complete the exchange. Every year, 15,000 Mexicans are killed in various disputes arising from this trade – the equivalent of all the Americans killed in Vietnam during the course of that war.

When he snorts that next line of cocaine, does the hipster really understand or even care that part of the price of that drug was a murdered Mexican: Some mother's son. A father's heir. Mexico's future.

Very Doubtful.

***

For almost a week, Tuma and I had gambled our way through the fields outside Holtville, a small agricultural town on the way to the East Border Crossing with Mexicali.

***

"Beautiful dog...that's a beautiful dog," Juan Diego said to Jesus who was busy consulting his cell phone for some particularly obscure information that only he would care about. "Yes and the big one – looks just like her but only three times as big and not nearly as pretty."

- Juan Diego was named for the humble farmer who encountered the Guadalupe Virgin, patron saint of most Mexicans and presented her to the bishop. Her likeness is all over our house in Indio and just about every other house, church – probably even cantinas throughout Mexico and La Frontera.

- Jesus was named, as you may have assumed, for Jesus. A lot of Mexican boys are. His full name was Jesus Carlos Gonzales. He was not named for Jesus Mal Verde, 19th century Robin Hood thug and patron saint of the Sinaloa Cartel and many other cartels.

Jesus then consulted his phone in response to Juan Diego's observation. He reported: "Yes, from all appearances, the first dog appears to be a Siberian Husky and the second, yes the second is a Malamute – they're both of the Spitz family and employed as sled dogs –the Siberian known for endurance and speed; the Malamute for strength."

"They are both ..."

"Enough information already Jesus," Juan Diego interrupted. "It looks like they're coming over to check us out. I hope they don't belong to some farmer or want to bite us. That big one looks hungry – the little one looks sneaky, kind of snippy."

***

I looked over the field – there were about six people – looked like my family back in Indio—who were busily picking something and these two odd balls who were standing around some distance away. One human– the little one – was drinking something out of a paper bag- and the second human – a big hairy one – was talking on a cell phone.

Tuma and I agreed that we should observe these humans more closely to see if they could become suitable travelling companions. As we approached the humans, I noticed that they had no shoes and were complaining about a coyote. I thought coyotes avoided humans: Did a coyote bite them or steal their food? I've seen them do that – once a pair of them tried to steal our food- that is until they came up against Tuma. Who took care of business, if you know what I mean.

But why weren't they wearing shoes? The big one has big hairy feet; the little one has tiny feet – maybe they don't need paw coverings?

"That darn coyote," I overheard the big one say. "We saved our money, hopped on the Beast at the Guatemala border, and survived the journey to the frontier. I remember some who didn't make it like Memo who lost both legs when he fell off and under the train or Rosa who ….It was horrible what they did to her. Such a nice woman, devoted wife and mother…"

"We even made it across the border in the back of that semi – never been so hot," Juan Diego added as he took another tug from his paper bag.

You shouldn't drink alcohol," Jesus interrupted. "It will impair your cognitive ability and ruin your liver. I only drink decaffeinated tea and abstain from caffeine…"

"And jelly donuts? Yea right, just tell me another story…" Juan Diego came back. "Traveling with you is enough to turn anybody into an alcoholic. Besides that my feet hurt."

"Mine too," Jesus replied. "Every Mexican mother tells her Mexican son that if he is going to ride the Beast to El Norte that he should put his money in his shoe. So, like every good Mexican son, I put my money in my shoe. And the first place the robbers looked – who like me also had Mexican mothers- was in my shoe. And stole all my money – that is what was left after that Coyote Mario Felix took his percentage."

"I was lucky to have the presence of mind to throw my cell phone away before they could steal that to," he concluded.

And Juan Diego chimed in," First they beat us up, then they made us take off our shoes and pull out the money and give it to them – then, and talk about insult to injury, they threw our shoes in the New River – a very sad end to my beautiful Nikes. Lucky I was able to hide my dear bottled friend here."

"Don't forget my Timberlands," Jesus added, "My leather shoes far exceeded your sneakers in quality and style. They will be sorely missed."

"So now, we're wandering around lost shoeless in some farmers field, and while the paisanos – our country men-won't turn us over to the migras they're not going to help us much either," Juan Diego complained.

"I think our coyote really foxed us – a coyote "foxed us –get it Juan Diego," Jesus asked.

"Of course I get it, you dork," Juan Diego returned. "Did you notice, how we were robbed before we got to the assigned motel? Remember how our Coyote said, "Wait at the motel until I get the signal to pick you up and get past the Border Patrol while they're between shifts."

"Yea, by the time we got to the motel, we were shoeless and money less – then they turned us away – I guess our credit wasn't very good. Sometimes, I just wish the migras would just pick us up and send us home," Jesus concluded.

"Me too," Juan Diego agreed and took another tug from the paper bag.

***

What do you feel about those guys," I asked Tuma. "Do you think that they would be good travelling companions? There are times when dogs need humans – if for nothing else than for companionship."

"I agree Tuma," said. "I know we have a well deserved reputation as killing machines, but we can also be compassionate especially when it comes to humans– and these guys could sure use help. A lot of it."

So we approached Jesus and Juan Diego. I went up to Jesus, rolled on my back – very carefully to cover my feminine parts with my tail – and Jesus found me irresistible. Most humans do.

Tuma was far less subtle than I and jumped up on Juan Diego knocking him down and licking his face. Juan Diego said some very bad words about doggie breath and struggled to free himself from my awesome friend. But he didn't really mean it.

"I think those dogs like us," Jesus said. "You know that they really look and act kind of like wolves. But they appear to be very affectionate."

"Chingado, too affectionate for me," Juan Diego added. I've still got dog babas all over me. I thought he'd never get off and stop licking my face. At least it was licking. Can you imagine the damage he could cause if he were biting instead?"

"The big male – he could be a big wolf – El Lobo; the little female, a little wolf, La Lobita. Nos Lobos – our wolves." Jesus observed.

"They'd make great travelling companions," Juan Diego added. "Nobody would mess with us with those two around –especially the big one."

At that time, we were heading south to rescue my humans; Jesus and Juan Diego were heading north on very sore feet to some imagined work in Indio. But I had the feeling that we would meet again and become fast friends and travelling companions.

***

Before I close this chapter, I need to relate something about Jesus. I knew he had cancer, which had already invaded and conquered his body. He would soon die. Perhaps my diagnosis of that dread disease had something to do with my superior sense of smell or some other quality of canine intuition.

I couldn't help but remember the dread and frustration I felt when Mom developed breast cancer. I smelled it, I tried my best to warn her – I danced around, barked and kept sniffing at her left breast – but it wasn't until the cancer spread that some human doctor recognized the problem and began the painful, dangerous and expensive process of pursuing a cure.

I knew months before the doctors did. The pain, the fear and danger of her illness would have been a morning in the hospital if Mom had just understood "dog." I've said it before and I'll say it again: Humans know so little about us and we know everything about them.

Chapter 3. Hermanos: Male and Female.
Santa Cruz to Calipatria

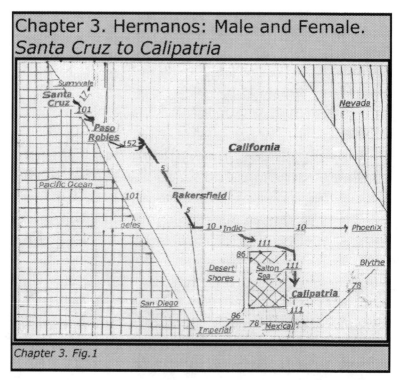

Chapter 3. Fig.1

Chapt.3.Fig1. Now, that's devotion. This is the map of Tuma's over 500-mile trip from Santa Cruz to help Courage. He couldn't have made it without the Jeden's help.

Chapter 3. Hermanos: Male and Female. *Calipatria to Brawley to Holtville.*

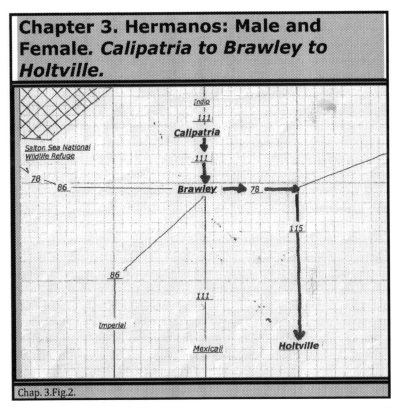

Chap. 3. Fig. 2.

We could have taken Rt 111 straight to downtown Mexicali but we decided to go out of our way and take the east Mexicali border crossing because it was safer and less crowded.

CHAPTER 4

THE BEAST

*Mexico is a peninsula punctuated by two large peninsulas –
Yucatan and Baja California. The Beast, the railroad made
famous in various movies such as Sin Nombre, folklore,
literature and music begins at the Guatemala border. The
Beast grows as it heads north toward the United States adding
tendrils to various border points stretching the equivalent of a
journey from Los Angeles to Chicago.*

*During the long slow and dangerous trip from south
to north, immigrants cling to the top, sides and even the
underneath couplings between cars: Accidents are common
and often deadly to the point where Mexican officials have
designated pickup truck driver-watchers to administer
first aid in case of accident. Charities also supply food and
emotional succor along the way to those who make the trip
and take the risk of leaving the Beast in hope of catching the
next train north.*

*Even more dangerous than the train, which heaves in fits
and starts at what seems at times to be its own logic, is human
predation where the stronger prey upon the weaker: Rape*

is every day, robbery more frequent and murder common. The narco traficantes also exploit the human cargo through intimidation and kidnapping where young men are persuaded to join the gangs, young women are forced into prostitution and old people are simply murdered. Yet the Beast grunts uncaring north insensitive to a passenger list of those seeking a better life in El Norte at whatever cost and at whatever risk.

***

East Border Crossing, Thursday, March 17, 2010.

Now St. Patrick's Day – maybe good for the Irish but bad for us Mexicans," Juan Diego griped.

"Catch and release, what am I, some kind of fish?" Juan Diego complained as he and Jesus hobbled back to the border under the watchful eye of Border Patrol. The migras had caught them in the U.S.; now it was time for border patrol to release them and send them back to Mexico their home country. At least they were not in some I.C.E prison.

"Besides that I'm embarrassed," Juan Diego, continued. "I borrowed all that money from friends and relatives and promised to pay it back when I got north and started earning the good Yankee dollar. Now they'll be on my case to pay it back for the rest of my natural life."

Although Juan Diego's hands were tied behind his back, Captain Gutierrez guided him toward the border with his hand on his shoulder in an almost fatherly fashion. Jesus wasn't as lucky: Officer Mount was rough almost to the point of brutality as they disembarked from the Border Patrol SUV.

I was both surprised and happy to see our human friends. I guess the Border Patrol caught them before they got to Indio. Still shoeless, Juan Diego was having the shakes and missing his bottle and Jesus was babbling away in Spanish to officer Mount who didn't understand a word he was saying. As we know, this migra doesn't speak "Mexican."

I sidled up to Jesus to keep a closer watch on Officer Mount to assure myself that he remained professional in his treatment of my friend. Humans- especially Jesus who was suffering from a nasal infection - can be so helpless. Like I noted previously, he also smelled of disease – much like Mom when she was diagnosed with cancer, but with Mom the cancer was located in one part of her breast while with Jesus the odor of cancer seemed to be all over his body.

If that wasn't bad enough, a large, raw-boned middle-aged white woman – strong on eye shadow and weak on deodorant – started screaming at Jesus from the window of her boat-sized Lincoln Town Car– yelling, "You're dirty. What's wrong with you? Clean up and get out of here."

She continued breathless with anger, "Your kind disgusts me. Where are your shoes? And who's that stupid little guy with you. Migras do your job."

"Do you know her," Juan Diego asked Jesus. "An old girl friend. You know, like hell hath no fury like a woman scorned."

"Never met her before," Jesus replied. "Give me some credit, I'm not the best looking guy in the world, far from macho and somewhat down on my luck right now, but I'm not that desperate."

I sure had my work cut out for me looking after Jesus: First Officer Mount and now this witch. All I could do was stick my face in her window and show her the teeth.

It worked. She muttered something like, "Dog" then screamed, "get out of my way. I'm off to see my children in Mexico." Squealed her tires and crashed into the curvy part of the border crossing– backed up and took off again south in a trail of dust, oil, cigarette smoke and profanity. The last word we heard from her was: "I'm Sycorax. Remember that name. We'll meet up again in Sinaloa."

***

It's often said, and with a great deal of justification, that going south is much easier than going north: When released by Border Patrol, Jesus and Juan Diego entered the never-never land between the two countries and emerged fed, clothed and yes, shoed by Mexican charity.

Good shoes yes, but the pants and shirts were somewhat dicey.

"Jesus," Juan Diego asked, "what do these shirts mean? Mine says Hollister. Is that somebody's name? And yours says Mel's' Dinner. Does that have something to do with food? My pants fit fine but yours barely reach to your knees – you look like a chollo, a middle aged teenager named for the cactus."

Jesus chuckled a reply and took great pride in knowing everything and if he didn't, just making it up. "Oh my little ignorant peones, my ignorant peasant," he said in a voice most redolent of a college professor he never had, "Hollister is a small town in California and Mel's Dinner is an elegant eating establishment in New York. The pants must have come from the same person. You and he must both be dreadfully short." Again, he was right – kind of.

"Jerk," Juan Diego, muttered admitting to himself that Jesus was indeed very smart and maybe he did know everything.

Although dusty and short of well-paid work, Mexico was home and they were glad to be back. "Once a Mexican, always a Mexican" Mexican President Calderon is reputed to have said. "You're always welcome home."

***

As noted previously, Tuma and I had chosen the East Border Crossing to Mexicali because it was less crowded and easier for us dogs and shoeless humans to navigate than the Central Border Crossing that empties right in the middle of the city.

The line of cars you see coming north at the Mexicali East Border Crossing represents a fraction of the 350 million legal border crossings a year made at the 45 official check points along the 1500 mile border between the United States and Mexico. Tuma and I followed a bunch of American tourists who were heading south to sample the food, the nightlife and, in some cases, get their teeth fixed in one of the cut rate dental clinics that line the border.

An aside: Mexicali also boasts some pretty good vets. I personally abhor that profession and those who practice it.

I did my beautiful dog thing while Tuma looked a little friendlier and less fearsome than was his usual demeanor. We were "Putting on the Dog" for the tourists. They bought it, and our crossing was eventful primarily for compliments and some food goodies.

***

Although little more than a line in the sand, the border between the two countries speaks to the power of water and those who control it.

The United States controls the headwaters of the Colorado River and its exploitation from the dry farms of the state of Colorado south through Arizona, Nevada and California enabling the economic ascendancy of this area of America known as the Sun Belt.

Those green fields just north of the border are fed by All American Canal, which exploits the last drop of potable water from the Colorado – a mighty river that no longer makes it to the sea. Even these green fields and the agricultural workers who work them are at risk as their owners chose the more profitable alternative of selling their water rights to feed the swimming pools and Florida palms of San Diego rather than the more tedious and chancy toil of the agricultural alternative.

***

The four of us were back together again walking along the dusty road from the Mexicali East Crossing to central city, the rail yards and the Beast. As is my fashion, I ran ahead – waited for the humans and Tuma to catch up – and then ran ahead again. The four of us slept just off the road to Mexicali in an abandoned shack – it smelled so bad that even the narco gangas couldn't stand staying there.

By going south we missed the human drama we would have seen going north. For over a mile before the Border Crossing, the roadside is littered with the hopes, dreams and desperation of those seeking what is euphemistically known as the entrepreneurial option.

Everything is for sale ranging from chewing gum, to velvet Elvises through graphic crucifixions. China is the country of origin for most of these plastic goodies; the purveyors of these items are mostly dark complected, small people from the extreme south of Mexico. These inheritors of the Pre-Columbian Mayan Empire appear to have ridden the Beast north but didn't quite make the border crossing with the United States.

Compassion for these people wars in the heart with the fatigue one experiences from a first person glimpse of so much of the world's suffering.

***

Indio, Friday, March 18

"I hate this bike. I just hate this bike. An old bicycle is no ride for a narco traficancte," Caleb stormed as he threw his bike down on the street and waited at the Indio McDonalds about five miles from his home in LaQuinta for a $25 bus ride south to Calexico. "I hope somebody steals it," he concluded.

The bus finally arrived. A few people got off – mostly aged Abualitas- and some got on – again mostly Abualitas. These Grand Mothers didn't seem to notice an angry, frightened young man who stormed his way to the back of the bus, his accustomed place on his ride to school.

Caleb wasn't much to look at: a slender young man – maybe 5'6" tall, fair skin marred by a constant eruption of acne and a slouch which only partially obscured a mal-developed shoulder. Dressed in saggy jeans practically down to his knees, an aggressive T shirt and heavily tattooed, his macho was fragile and his fears obvious. Most of his earthly possessions – IPod, Cell Phone, change of clothes and some cookies – were at his feet in an old gym bag – the subject of much ridicule in class.

The bus rumbled along #86 to #111 and seemed to stop at every large and small town on its way to Calexico. The anguished questions of a young woman who needed to get from the turnoff at the Border Patrol Station on #86 to Borrego Springs awakened him from his funk and set his adolescent mind to thinking about gangs and girls.

Caleb hadn't had much success with either: Not macho enough for the gangs and too ugly and poor for the girls. He favored the Latinas- short and round – who either ignored him or ridiculed his deformity. His fantasies turned to a teacher – a blond, thin blue-eyed goddess – who was actually nice to him – and patient as he struggled through beginning algebra. He would be her protector, her caballero -her knight in shining armor. The physical stuff he'd hold for the short, round ones.

Caleb went in and out of sleep and fantasy as the bus finally ground to a welcome stop in Calexico – a small American town of about 38,000 nestled on the Mexican border just north of the sprawling industrial hub of Mexicali, a city bursting with 1 million plus inhabitants.

After a welcome box of fried chicken at Churches on the American side, Caleb crossed the border on foot and decided to share a dollar cab with three other people to go the five miles to the Mexicali central bus station. After a short wait at the station, he boarded the bus for the 18-hour plus ride to Culiacan - cost of about $185. He took the money for the bus fare out of his shoe plus some extra for food, goodies and bribes, expenses which he would incur during the trip. Sycorax, his Mom, had given him enough money to make the trip plus what little he had remaining from the robbery. Where his Mom got her money from was a mystery he chose not to solve.

As they pulled out of the station, Caleb noticed a marked change in the complexion of the passengers: Yes, there were still any numbers of Abualitas but in addition to grandmothers there were students and mixed ages ranging from squalling babies to old men in reverie. The bus – "Transportes del Pacific"- was filled with people who did not have the money to travel by air or car. Rail, known as the Beast, had long been freight only. Some of the passengers were just traveling locally or had too much baggage to carry on a plane.

Important cities along the way to Culiacan included Hermosillo, Sonora and Obregon, Sonora. At these stops the travelers could anticipate a 30-minute wait – time to stretch their legs and feast upon the local cuisine. In between Hermosillo and Obregon, a pretty young girl sat next to Caleb and seemed to be interested in pursuing friendship, but he denied her much conversation ascribing her attraction to his American citizenship. He didn't want a Green Card marriage.

To interdict drug, gun and cash smuggling, the Mexican government has instituted two stops along the way to Culiacan: Sonoyta, Sonora and further south, San Emeterio,

Sonora. Unfortunately, corruption has infected this process and the passengers are requested to "dame algun dinero para los refrescos." Literally translated this expression means, "Give me some money for soda." Depending on the inspector and the passenger, it can cost from one to ten dollars to satisfy the officer's thirst. Caleb got stuck for $10 – although fluent in Spanish, he looked American.

***

MEXICALI, FRIDAY, MARCH 18

"My feet hurt, I'm thirsty and I don't think we'll ever get there," Juan Diego complained as the four of us walked along the highway west to downtown Mexicali. I couldn't help but agree: My paws were made for snow, grass and the finer things of life – not hot asphalt. It looked like Jesus and Tuma were of the same mind. An hour's walk got us no closer to Mexicali than the creeping tendrils of row houses that appear to grow out of its center city core and evolve toward the east border crossing.

Our journey would run through the city to the working class near suburbs and to the rail yards in the industrial section on the western side of town. Ferromex runs a freight line from Mexicali to Calexico but the line is so heavily guarded that it makes hitching a ride virtually impossible. It looked to be a long, hot, dry and noisy trip to get to the Beast.

***

A little about Mexicali – a sprawling city of some one million plus Mexicans living directly to the south of the U.S. border and Calexico.

A young town, founded around the beginning of the twentieth century, Mexicali is the capital of the state of California Baja and a leading industrial and agricultural center. An adolescent major city, its population has soared to over a million within the last two decades. Boasting the Silicon Border with industrial giants such as Kenworth, Hitachi and Sony, it sits astride the major trade routes between Mexico and the United States. Although they value their jobs and make hard working and tractable employees, many can be heard to complain that their factories offer Mexican wages at an American cost of living.

Founded in concert with Calexico (California-Mexico), its American sister city, Mexicali (Mexico-California) had to import its first inhabitants. It was the Chinese who arrived in San Felipe, a fishing village along the Gulf of California about south of Mexicali. They were tricked into the long 100 mile trip north from San Felipe to what was to become Mexicali. They appeared to be the only ethnic group that had the stamina and willingness to withstand the withering desert heat – which blisters at over a hundred degrees most summer, early fall and late spring days.

The Chinese legacy remains in any number of excellent restaurants that dot the city, and in Cerro del Chinero (Chinese Hill) where upwards of 100 Chinese died of thirst and exposure less than 30 miles north of San Felipe on their way to Mexicali.

Although far from boasting European standards of clean air and water-even the air smells of the work of past sulfur belching steel plants- Mexicali's electrical generation is green and supplied by a large complex of geothermal stations fed by the Cerro Prieto volcano. A dormant bump less than 100 feet high in the desert landscape approximately south of Mexicali, this unprepossessing geothermal heat source has been supplying 80% of all electricity to Baja California Sur and surrounding areas for the past 40 years.

Mexicali grows on the Colorado River flood plain whose delta recently equaled the expanse and fertility of the Nile before the Americans dammed upriver. The devastation caused by the strangulation of the Colorado River can be seen most graphically when you look east to the Gulf of California from route five on the road to San Felipe, a Mexican fishing village and an American tourist destination south of Mexicali: There is nothing but salt flats totally devoid of life: Not even a creosote bush. Nothing for five miles to the sea. Nothing where dolphins used to play.

Mexicali relies on water from what's left of the Colorado River and a rapidly diminishing aquifer. Every day, drinking water is delivered by truck in well-used plastic containers to your door. If you can pay for it. Bottled water is only slightly less dangerous than the stuff that comes out of the tap.

***

CULIACAN, SATURDAY, MARCH 19

For Caleb, the bus seemed to take forever to arrive. Eighteen hours is a longtime for anybody especially a teenage boy riding on a bus, plagued by raging hormones, fears, hopes and fantasies. Caleb woke up, stretched, rubbed his eyes and saw Mexico-not the frontera of industrial Mexicali, the danger of Tijuana or the drug war induced devastation of Ciudad Juarez – but Culiacan – a beautiful city approaching a million in population, agricultural-industrial center, capital of Sinaloa and home of the dreaded Sinaloa cartel.

Settled by the Spanish in the late 16th century, Culiacan was an established town well before the English pilgrims set foot on Plymouth Rock. Built where the Tamazulat and Humaza Rivers join, the Culiacan River is spanned by nine bridges and boasts a railhead, international airport and access to the Pan American highway. For tourists, the best place to see the city is from the Templo de Nuestra Senora de Guadalupe- the historical religious center which remains the downtown Cathedral.

Caleb was neither interested in religious architecture nor had the time for sports so he plunged into the crowded downtown of Rosales Street and ate his fill of the local cuisine treating himself to Camarones en agua chile, a regional specialty, while ogling the local senoritas – who as usual failed to ogle back. The forty-mile trip by local bus to El Dorado and the anxiety of meeting his uncle would come soon enough.

***

And so it did: The slow, bumpy bus ride from Culiacan finally ground to an end in El Dorado. Now at the bus station the best Caleb could do was wait around – his cell phone didn't work, and he was at a loss as to where to go and what to do until a dark, short, broad shouldered man appeared and motioned him to the back of a battered pickup truck. They rode about five miles to a complex of four, gray, poured concrete buildings roughly arranged in a square with a cemetery on one side and cornfields on the other three. The door to the complex was heavy reinforced steel and well guarded by at least six, silent well-armed men. The man motioned Caleb to what appeared to be some kind of office where he was to meet his uncle Antonio.

"I'm not your uncle," the man said to Caleb after what felt like an hour's wait. "Uncle is a courtesy title foisted on me by your mother – my mother in law. I'm married to her daughter and your half sister Priscilla who is appreciably better looking and a lot smarter than you are."

"You will call me Patron,' he went on. "Do you see that Escalade? Clean it. If you do a good enough job we can see about some dinner. Get to work. Good by."

And, as so instructed, Caleb went to work.

***

Mexicali, Friday, March 18

"I'm hot, dog-tired, hungry and just plain miserable," I said to myself. "So I'm just going to sit down right here and not put another paw to the street. This isn't like home where, when it was hot, I could stand in my pool, kick the water up to my tummy; dig a hole in the nice warm dirt and chase around the house spreading mud all over the place. Mom would get mad at Dad and say "Your Dog," but I knew they really weren't angry." I just sat down and wouldn't move.

After a while the rest of our troupe weakened on our journey toward the bowels of Mexicali: First Tuma sat down and then Jesus and Juan Diego joined him. We'd probably still be sitting there starving to death, bitten by fleas and slowly desiccating in the desert sun, if Bill, a nice old American guy driving a old white Chevy pickup heavily used and almost as old as he was, hadn't stopped. "Beautiful Dog" he called out to me. Then I knew that we had a ride.

"OK," he said, "what do you call yourselves." Jesus and Juan Diego answered with their names. He replied, "Not you humans, idiots, the dogs." Jesus answered, "the big one we call, Lobo – Spanish for wolf;" Juan Diego chimed in with "The little one, the Beautiful Dog, we call Lobita which is Spanish for little, female wolf. We don't know their real names."

"Get in the truck, I'll get you to the close-in industrial suburbs and then you'll have to paw it to the rail-yards. Not so fast, humans, dogs in the front seat; humans in the back," he concluded.

I knew I was going to like this guy – he had his priorities right: Although as we drove, I had to remind him that he had to keep one hand free – that hand was for me. After a long time with Tuma, Juan Diego and Jesus, I needed some serious affection and petting in the extreme.

As we drove toward the city center, I kept remembering various landmarks and came to the startling conclusion that we were going to go right past my Abualita's, Mom's mother's, house and home and resting place to various other relatives too numerous to count.

A high cement wall covered at the top by broken glass surrounded her house like all the others on that street and throughout Mexicali. The front of each house boasts a stout iron gate. To an American dog, walking down the street faced with locked iron gates and topped by cement walls was like walking the hall between the cells of a maximum-security prison except the good guys are locked in cells behind iron gates while the bad guys roam outside. Kind of like a kennel.

Unlike American gated communities with their voice activated gates and easily scaled walls, the houses in Mexicali were of various sizes and degrees of elegance. None of the tedious uniformity of American planned communities was to found here. Some houses stretched for three building lots with all the blessings of gardens and professional masonry located right next to humble house on one lot with far less ornament or finished work.

Bill dropped us off right in front of my Abualita's house with word that he had to see his mother in law about some something important – maybe the kidnapping," I thought.

Just as we were getting out of the truck, Loraina, Mom's' niece called out to me, "Courage it's you," she called.

"Who did she think it was," I thought. "I wanted out of there, fast and for good reason: I admitted to myself, "OK, I in a brief moment, I bit her daughter – I don't know why. She was a nice girl. I guess I was just cranky. For that very good reason I was not Ms. Popularity in her neighborhood."

All three of my companions, called out to me "Hey Lobita, these people know you. Maybe we can get something good to eat? Or drink? Or maybe a nap on something soft? Even the garbage looks good."

***

Mexicali to Culiacan, Saturday, March 19 – Wednesday March 23.

Please note that it would take our four heroes to ride three Beasts (the north-south freight trains) to get from Mexicali to Culiacan.

"Sorry guys," I barked out. "We need to get moving. Can't miss the train."

Our goal was the Beast – or actually the Beasts – a series of freight trains that went from the US. –Mexican border to Guatemala. Going north it was crowded – human beings on the top, sides, and couplings and even underneath the train. For us, however, the trip was pretty easy. We were going south and practically had the trains all to ourselves.

Between you and me, the last thing I wanted to do was stay with my in laws – my biting thing had seriously damaged that relationship.

I had to run ahead and back again four times just to get the three of them moving – out of that neighborhood and on to the train. It was a rough trip and I must admit that, in this instance, the humans were a big help in getting us across some very big, noisy honking streets crowded by a million seriously insane drivers who appeared intense on running us over – that is, if they had any thoughts at all.

In the rail yards, caution preceded valor. Dad had told me that a long time ago when he rode the rails with the tramps, they told him to wait for a boxcar with both doors open before he climbed on board. One door open would be for insurance. If one door closed, you would still have one door open for your escape. If by accident both doors closed, you might well anticipate a very slow, painful death by starvation.

Scream as you might, sound wouldn't penetrate those thick wooden walls, and, even if it did, there would be nobody to hear you.

Rail yards are so confusing: Which way do the rails run? Are those boxcars going some place or just sitting there? Is the train going to switch left or right? And I knew that those steel unfeeling monsters would kill you without a bit of remorse. Again our human companions came in handy: Juan Diego shared a beer with one of the railroad police and Jesus asked directions. They got us on a boxcar with both doors open (Dad would be very proud of me) and some food and drink. Tuma and I easily jumped in the car; Juan Diego followed. Jesus had some problem but we got him in. The car was completely empty except for a sack of beans in the corner.

It seemed forever while the train formed up – jerking when a group of cars coupled on – then doing nothing – then another bang and jerk and we were moving.

***

Bouncing down along the way on the Beast to Culiacan, Jesus began singing. It went like this:

"I've been working on the railroad all the livelong day. I've been working on the railroad just to pass the time away... Can't you hear the whistle blowing ..."

"Not bad for a human," I barked to Tuma. "Jesus could sing in the St. Thomas choir under the direction of that nice lady Pat.

Then Juan Diego started to make noises that he thought were singing. "No, Juan Diego, not so fast," I barked out at him. "Have a drink. Go to sleep. Like my Dad would say, "You can't carry a tune in a bucket."

Tuma and I agreed that Jesus was ok –for a human that is. But then we decided to show those humans what singing was really all about: I started our duet with a full measure soprano howl and worked my way down the scale to bass with a series of sharp quarter note barks. Tuma followed me up the scale beginning in a series of grunts – acting as a basso continuo- gradually increasing the tempo and volume until we met at a mutual baritone bark that lasted a full measure at C. I ended our song with a series of muffled sounds in my throat. Tuma completed the duet with a counter tenor howl that shook the train.

"Now, my human friends, that's singing."

The sound of wheels on rails and the groan of the car as it swayed slowly on poorly maintained track was a soporific: Men and dogs were soon asleep. I saw Tuma twitch a little and then his legs broke into a run – I wonder if he was downing an elk or running from an angry farmer. Juan Diego snored; Jesus talked in his sleep about computers.

***

El Dorado, Sunday March 20.

While we were sleeping and singing on the train, Caleb was in his uncle's complex about five miles outside El Dorado, Mexico getting to know his Uncle Antony just a little bit better.

"Clean it again," Antonio growled at Caleb. It was late and Caleb was tired, hungry and frightened by this man who said little and seemed to control all. "Si Patron," Caleb said to his uncle and cleaned the Escalade again.

"Give the kid some beans," Antonio said to his wife Priscilla after Caleb had cleaned the car to his satisfaction. We're running short on cash and can't afford the meat for carne asada."

"Tomorrow, Caleb I'm going to give you an assignment. You can sleep in the bunkhouse tonight with Jorge. Stephano has his own room," he said and went back to his office.

"Maybe this guy isn't so bad after all," Caleb said to himself and looked around for some straw and well used blankets to get through the night.

EL DORADO, MONDAY, MARCH 21.

Morning dawned in darkness. "Vamos muchacho" – with these words Jorge dragged Caleb out of his makeshift bed to tell him that El Patron had his assignment. "Second day on the job and the boss has something for me to do. This should be exciting," he thought a little anxiously.

Once in his office, Antonio said to him: "Your English is pretty good so I'm going to have you work a little with our honored guests – the old Americans we picked up when you told us about their winnings. With the million dollars you told us about still hung up in process, we haven't been able to set up a proper procedure for getting the ransom."

"I want you to get the debit card and code for his bank account from the old man," he went on. "Americans always keep a high balance in their checking. When you get the card and the code, I want you to drive into El Dorado, go to Banco National and clean him out. Bring a receipt. I want every peso. I mean what I say. Don't forget it."

As he left the office, Caleb felt pretty good. Getting the information from the old man shouldn't be much trouble. If he did give him any trouble, he was sure he could rough him up a bit to get what he needed. The couple was housed in a room less than 100 yards away from where Antonio lived and worked.

"Hey you," Caleb shouted to Dad, the old man, when he got to their room. "Give me your debit card and your code. And be quick about it."

The old man stood up and asked Caleb what he wanted.

"Your debit card," you idiot," Caleb responded.

Caleb then grabbed the old man by the shoulder. "Look you son of a ...I want your card and I want it now," he screamed at the old man.

"Please take your hands off me and watch your language," the old man replied.

"Are you kidding me, you old fool," Caleb shouted.

In a flash, the old man sharply raised his knee into the young man's groin. As the young man groaned down in pain, the old man grabbed him by the hair and forced his face into the hard cement floor. He then took the young man's arm and bent it up his back.

"You mother..." Caleb screamed.

"Language ...language," the old man retorted.

"Corazon, you're going to break his arm or dislocate his shoulder," his wife reminded him. "I plan to," the old man said and raised the young man's arm a little higher. More screams.

With a pop of torn ligaments and pulled tendons, the old man dislocated the young man's shoulder. More screams. Between tears of pain and fear of more to come, Caleb begged for mercy.

"OK. But now hold on," the old man said. "This is going to hurt even more. I'm going to relocate your shoulder. And, by the way, in the future, call me sir." The old man pulled the young man's arm full length and jerked his shoulder back into place. The pain burned through his body but Caleb bore it – no tears or screams this time no matter how much it hurt.

Still sore and aching, Caleb asked the old man how he learned to fight like that.

"In the army," he replied.

"Did you kill anybody, the young man asked?

"No, fortunately not. I was a medic, but before medical training all of us had to go through basic training where we were taught all sorts of ways to kill and maim people– including what I just did to you," he concluded.

"Sir, I really need your credit card and code," Caleb asked virtually pleading for mercy. "If I don't get the money, my uncle will kill me."

The old man gave him the card and code. "Remember, he concluded, "we're still waiting for the state to break loose with the money – one million big ones. It should be here any time."

After Caleb left, Mom said, "Corazon, you know there is no money."

"I know that," the old man said. "I was just buying time on credit."

Saturday, March 23 – Wednesday, March 29. Between Mexicali and Culiacan

Still on the train, the four of us heard the unmistakable sound of: "Fwap...rrrip..craack...ah..."

"It must be the dogs, Juan Diego said to Jesus.

"Pow...pop...poom." And "ah" again...

"Yea, that's right. They always blame the dog," I said to Tuma.

And out of a fowl smelling greenish haze appeared Ariel Rabinowitz, Conductor and Ticket Taker, dressed in a brass buttoned blue suit and shiny well-worn blue trousers.

"Tickets please ...Tickets please for the Beast, the train to hell."

"Did you make that awful smell and blame it on us dogs," I shot back.

"She who smelt dealt," the Jeden returned.

"Well," I said, "it wasn't me who dealt. Now will you please stick your luminescence out the door before we all suffocate."

"You dogs can be so insensitive. I told you everything about myself: How I am neither plant nor animal; the complicated science of my luminescence; my expiration date and conflict with my replacement unit. OK, I dodged the stuff about my religion."

"But," with his voice rising in pain and anguish at the insensitivity of all dogs and humans, "did you ever ask me or even care what I like to eat. No. Did you have any idea that I just love to eat - Beans? "Beans ...beans...the musical fruit, the more you eat, the more you... Here, grab my finger."

"That is enough," I shot back. "I will not have bathroom humor on my train."

"Bossy...bossy alpha female," the Jeden replied. "Beans... beans are good for your heart...the more you eat...the more you..."

"Now Jeden, just cool it with the bean stuff," I reminded him.

***

As we talked, the car darkened and Tuma, Jesus and Juan Diego drifted into the shadows as the Jeden's conversation turned serious, almost mournful. The Jeden addressed me exclusive of the others. As the Jeden talked, my angel, my friend Ariel Rabinowitz, morphed from train conductor to prophet – not the joyful Isaiah but more the censorious Jeremiah.

"Just trying to add a little to humor to a very difficult situation," the Jeden said in hushed tones. "This is truly the train to hell. Hell will begin in El Dorado and flourish in the near countryside."

"You will lose friends. You will see humans at their worst: Torture and the murder of innocents. You will earn your name Courage through tears and pain. Be brave, my friend, be smart and earn your true wolf," the Jeden concluded - only to add:

"You know, I really do like beans," the Jeden said and disappeared.

Culiacan, Wednesday March 23.

The train finally ended its forever journey to Culiacan. Tuma and I got off first, followed by Juan Diego. Jesus was last to leave and said while he eased out of the train to Juan Diego, "do you remember the sack of beans?"

"Yes, I do, Juan Diego replied. "That sack of beans brought back memories of home and Mamacita's beans. Her beans, soaked and cooked for what seemed a day then mashed with just the right amount of pork fat – no wonder the Jeden loves beans. Mamacita's were the best."

"My friend," Jesus retorted, "your Mamacita's beans may have been good ...maybe even great, but nothing compares with my Mom's. Her beans – well she did all the right stuff –soaking, boiling and pork fat – but she had a secret stash of chilies that made her beans the greatest."

Why do you think that the Americans call Mexicans "Beaners," when they want us to feel bad ...like wetbacks ...feel like less than we are," Juan Diego asked.

"Beats me," Jesus answered. "Calling me a Beaner seems more of a complement than an insult."

Well, my friend, remember that sack of beans, well it's not there anymore. Completely gone." Juan Diego noted.

***

El Dorado, Monday, March 21.

What happened back there," Antonio asked. "I heard a lot of noise – some screams of pain. You look really flushed. Does your shoulder hurt? I hope you didn't harm our honored guests too badly. They're our trip to Cancun and retirement."

"Patron, I didn't hurt them very much– not to see anyway. The old man gave me a little trouble. So I had to persuade him, if you know what I mean."

"I do know what you mean," Antonio answered. "You have real potential in the family business. Now get in the truck and head to El Dorado and get the money out of the bank to tide us over until the big stuff comes in."

"Well, maybe El Patron is not so bad at all," Caleb, said to himself as he left the office and got into the truck. "He wouldn't give me the Escalade – can't hurt for asking –but I did get to drive the truck which sure beats that horrible old bike I left in Indio."

"There's only one problem. I don't know how to drive stick shift," he thought, "but no way am I going to tell El Patron – or anybody else – that I don't know how to drive this vehicle."

With his mind racing back to driver's ed. at Indio High School, Caleb remembered: "First you start the engine. No. It won't start – well it tried to but only jerked and then stopped. Oh, yes, push in the clutch – the peddle on the right side – or was it the left. No, the clutch is on the left. Push it down and start the engine. Good. The engine started. Now, let out the clutch. Too soon. It stalled. Keep the clutch in and put it in first gear- yea, that's right, the gears are like an H. Stalled again. Let the clutch in gradually.

The car bucked; lurched, and stalled out a few times before he got out of the compound and onto the street. While the truck was moving, the gears were pretty easy to move up. He didn't try to down shift, and he dreaded stopping: "Now remember, depress the brake on the right and the clutch on the left and ease off on the accelerator." And then he had to remember the whole thing about starting again: "Let out the clutch – not too slow or the engine would roar and tires would squeal or too fast and the truck would stall."

Reverse was just beyond him. After he got within walking distance of town, he parked the truck nose out- that way, when he needed to leave and go back to the compound, he wouldn't have to engage in the struggle to master the mystery of the reverse gear.

Parking a good 15-minute walk from town, Caleb asked around to find El Banco National. There was a lot of advice and as many banks as advice so he went to the first one he found. "I hope the old man gave me the right code. Oh yes, he did. Must have been afraid of El Patron. This is much easier than driving that stupid truck," he thought as he put in the card and the code. The ATM seemed to think a while and then wiky...wiky ...wiky and out came the money. Just like magic.

Caleb counted out $3,104.12. He'd never seen so much money. Americans did keep high balances. Don't forget what El Patron said: "Keep a receipt and bring every peso. Or something very bad will happen." Well, not wanting anything bad to happen, he pocketed the receipt and rounded off the amount – El Patron would never notice - $3,000 in his shoe for his uncle and $104.12 for himself.

As they say– "a fool and his money are soon parted." To be sure, Caleb found a way to be a fool and part with his money – the cantina was right next to the bank, and he quickly availed himself of its services. Without even a wink of the eye or request for identification, the bar tender filled his request for a beer and charged twice the going rate. Three, or was it four beers, went down very quickly. And he soon changed to Margaritas – one Margarita, two Margaritas...

He never got to three, four- just very close until the bartender cut him off. In the process of getting very drunk, an attractive woman, heavily made up, short of dress and long on cleavage, asked if he would "like to have a good time. I work for your uncle. I think we can deal."

Who wouldn't want to have a good time especially with this gorgeous senorita," he thought as alcohol-trumped hormones and he fell face down with his head on the bar. The bar tender threw him out on the street while he and the senorita relieved him of what money he still had in his pockets. They left his shoes in tact. Didn't want to be greedy.

***

Drunk and stupid, Caleb got into the truck – the whole thing about standard shift was so difficult that is seemed almost easier to drive drunk. He lurched it and stalled it, left the road a few times but somehow he and the truck made it back to the compound. A very angry Patron was waiting.

"Three hours late and drunk out of your mind," El Patron observed. "I don't care where you have been or what you've been doing but I want the money. I want all of it and I want it now. With the receipt."

Caleb pulled off his shoe, dug around in his sock for the money and laid out $3,000 on the desk. He found the receipt somewhere in a pocket and put it next to the money.

With his voice barely a whisper, Antonio said to Caleb "let me repeat what I told you earlier: When you get the card and the code, I want you to drive into El Dorado, go to Banco National and clean him out. Bring a receipt. I want every peso. I mean what I say. Don't forget it."

"I see a receipt for $3,104.12 and cash for $3,000. If my math is correct – and I assure you that it is –we have $104.12 missing. Where is it? Am I missing something?"

"But uncle – I mean Patron – I thought you wouldn't miss the little extra," Caleb slurred out.

"Oh, but I do. You've made me very unhappy. People do not steal or lie to me if they anticipate dying old and surrounded by loving relatives. I would have Jorge –yes the broad shouldered man you met in El Dorado – the quiet man who drove you here – end your pathetic little life with a surfeit of pain and anguish."

"But I won't- not this time – because I don't want to listen to all the noise and grief from your mother my beloved mother in law Sycorax- who would suddenly remember how much she loved you. So I'll have Jorge here assist me while I give you a remembrance. Something to think about every time you shake hands, pick your nose or wipe your..."

Jorge appeared silently and apparently out of nowhere. At Antonio's request he took Caleb's right wrist and wrestled it down to his boss's desk and held it there.

"Spread your fingers, Caleb," Antonio said and pulled his knife from his boot and placed it on the young man's pinkie finger between his second and third knuckle.

With the knife in his right hand, Antonio fisted his left hand and slammed it down on the knife. It cut half way through the bone. A second time and it severed the bone and with the third blow he sliced the remaining skin. Caleb fainted. Jorge kicked him awake, and the young man screamed, cried and staggered out of the office.

Jorge took the remains of the young man's finger, held it in the air and laughing asked "did your forget something?"

What a mess," Antonio complained, "blood everywhere - all over my desk. The desk my beloved mother gave me when I was in seminary. Plus that idiot kid's finger. I should have had Jorge dispose of that nuisance kid. Now I'm practically sick with all this gore."

His wife, Priscilla who had thrilled to whole scene, said "Why don't you send the finger to the DeLeon's with a reminder that there will be more body parts to come if they don't hurry up with the money," she suggested. "Who's to know who belonged to this nasty, bloody finger? Could be the old man's for all anybody would know."

"Good idea. Should speed the process along. Free for nothing. I'll have Stephano drop it off in the Deleon's mailbox on his next trip to El Norte," Antonio agreed. He usually agreed with Priscilla, his wife, and mother of his children, confidante and bookkeeper.

✳✳✳

In a Friday, March 26 E-mail

To Sheradino Deleon from Agent MacDuff: "I wouldn't worry about the finger – it's not your Mom's or your Dad's but belongs to our little narco traficante wannabe Caleb. Showed up in the finger print database – didn't even have to do DNA lab work. How he lost it is anybody's' guess.

The amateurishness of this whole operation worries me: First they haven't given us a time or place to deliver the ransom and now there is this business with a severed finger. Their lack of experience in the process and exchange of kidnap and ransom is a cause for concern – they could panic and kill your loved ones. And, like I've said before, there will be no SEALS, drones or black helicopters – Mexicans are very jealous of their sovereignty and would not tolerate American interference.

However, the most important word in FBI is Intelligence and I have some information regarding the situation on the ground. I did my two-year service in this area of Mexico and actually know some of the principals:

Antonio is the leader and runs a very tight ship. We go back a long way and I thought I knew him well – apparently I was in error. When he was in seminary and I was performing my missionary work, the two of us had numerous and passionate discussions well into the night arguing the relative merits of Roman Catholicism and the Church of Jesus Christ of the Latter Day Saints. No booze just a lot of ice tea to fuel our arguments. I was sure he would have his own parish by now and not be running a second rate criminal enterprise. I don't know where things went wrong.

The others include his brother Stephano who, because of some minor birth defect, is "slow" - not retarded but definitely not all there. The defect is probably a result of poor or lack of prompt medical care at birth. Could have been me if our doctor hadn't intervened with an emergency Caesarian. Antonio is very protective of him, and Stephano is devoted to his big brother.

Jorge is Antonio's enforcer. A sadistic thug of uncertain origin, he proudly wears #13 and is said to be a devote of Santa Muerte and Jesus MalVerde. Priscilla is Antonio's wife, a Mexican-American of uncertain Eastern-European heritage and daughter of Sycorax who is on our watch list of narco traficantes. It is said that mother and daughter are the source of Antonio's ambition.

We're going to have to move quickly on this one. It's my guess that your father in law has been delaying the process of ransom. Clever old guy, but time is running out. I won't go into any details but I hope to have this operation wrapped up in a week. It will be sudden and extremely violent. Pray God your Mom and Dad survive it. There are no guarantees. Stay close but stay away. Be prepared for a happy reunion or a tragic funeral.

Yours, Agent MacDuff

PS. I got your note about Courage and her human and canine entourage. They appear to have made the border crossing at the East Gate and made it to the Mexicali Rail Yards.

Did that dog read <u>Call of the Wild</u> or did she write it?

Chapter 4. The Beast. *Indio to Mexicali to Culiacan*.

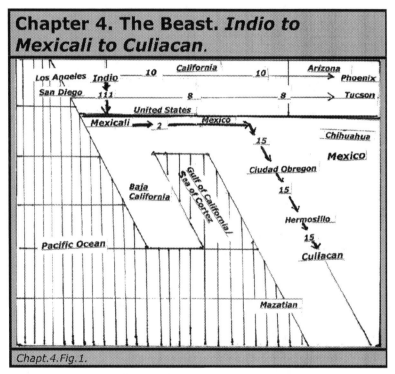

Chapt.4.Fig.1.

Follow us as we travel from Holtville to the East Border Crossing where we hooked up with Jesus and Juan Diego. From there we went to the Mexicali Train yards and the Beast.

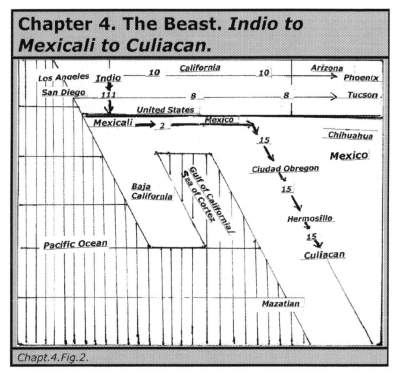

Chapt.4.Fig.2.

Although the means of travel was different – Caleb by bus and the four of us by Beast, we all ended up in Culiacan on our way to the narco traficannte's hideout near El Dorado.

Chapter 4. The Beast. *Culiacan to El Dorado.*

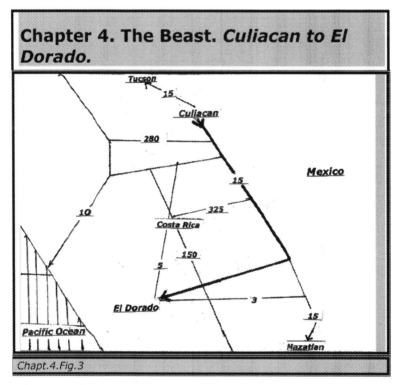

Chapt.4.Fig.3

The map shows our progress from Culiacan to El Dorado.

CHAPTER 5

THE CACTUS SMILED: PART 1

When the Spanish conquered Mexico City, they were amazed at the size and complexity of that metropolis and how it exceeded Madrid in splendor and sophistication. Spanish steel, cunning and germs quickly conquered Mexico replacing a cruel religion with a gentle faith whose followers were as brutal as any Aztec and whose diseases decimated the native population.

The genes of the new and old peoples as well as their native and European backgrounds blended to form a vibrant Mestizo culture. Two cultural icons exemplify this ethnic mixing: Guadalupe Virgin- who is said to be a Christian iteration of the Aztec mother goddess and whose likeness may be found in every God fearing Mexican home and Santa Muerte – the Aztec goddess of death and Jesus Mal Verde, the Narco Saint – both favorites of Narco Traficantes.

Although blessed in many ways, Mexico is also cursed with two warring factions: The central government versus the narco traficantes. This political, economic and cultural bifurcation *is putting the country at risk of failure as it moves toward first world status. Supported by money and guns from its neighbor to the north, two of the major players in this deadly drama – Los Zetas and the Sinaloa Cartel – continue their bloody fight for control of the lucrative drug trade routes from Latin America to the United States.*

Beginning in the 1960s, the Sinaloa Cartel has grown to become the largest drug trafficking organization in the world and now controls much of 17 Mexican states. Santo Jesus Mal Verde (not accepted as a saint by the Catholic church), known as a Robin Hood and killed in 1909, is a hometown hero. Los Zetas, a relative newcomer to the conflict, was begun in 1999 by a dissident group of Mexican Special Forces based in Nuevo Laredo. Regarded as the most dangerous and technologically sophisticated of all the players in this gruesome war, they control 11 Mexican states and are contesting control of Sinaloa territory.

Mexico's President Calderon led the effort to wrest control of the country from the narco traficantes by the legally established central government. Army troops, masked and recruited from disparate parts of the country, continue to war with various Cartels. The results are mixed: The central government has decimated the Cartel's armies but they still control much territory and can strike with impunity wherever and when ever they choose. Spreading the terror nationwide, the 15,000 tortured dead a year includes, not only the mutilated remains of Cartel soldiers, but also those of innocent farmers and journalists alike. The country cries for an end to the violence. Now President Nieto promises "a kinder gentler" approach to the narco wars. We can only wish him well.

With recent capture of El "Chapo" Guzman, the Sinaloa Cartel has been dealt a serious setback in its drive for complete dominance of the international drug trade with business all the way to downtown Chicago and Europe. A local illiterate boy born of poor family, El Chapo (Shorty Guzman) became one of the richest men in the world and seen by many in Sinaloa as a hero –a Robin Hood who supported local charities and remained hidden in the Sinaloa hills by friends and family. Others feared him; many hated him for the brutality meted out to those who contest his will. A visiting tourist to Mazatlan, where the drug king was on vacation, wouldn't even notice that he was there.

When arrested by the Mexican Marines with an assist from the Americans, the feared El Chapo appeared nothing but a little man held at the neck by a masked soldier - an unprepossessing crook on his way to prison. The question of extradition remains moot: the Americans want him to try him to assure that he does not escape from prison as he did once before in a laundry truck. Mexicans want to try and punish him out of national integrity and the unspoken fear that many of those in power would be compromised through the tentacles of corruption.

In addition to Guzman's arrest, the Zetas, a feared competitor have been weakened by the capture of some of their top leadership and the Knights Templar, who held a stranglehold on the Mexican state of Michoacán, have been seriously weakened by a local vigilante group – impatient for national recognition of their issues. However, as long as El Norte has the money and desire for drugs, there will be a need and those who will fill that need no matter the cost in blood and treasure.

***

In this chapter of *Courage* we follow the progress and demise of a fictional Cartel – El Simba- a newcomer to the brutal contest for control of a significant piece of the national and international criminal action. Built on extortion and prostitution in their El Dorado hometown, El Simba attempts to raise money through a mistaken foray into the profitable business of kidnapping. While the big dogs - Sinaloa Cartel, Los Zetas, Knights Templar and others - are otherwise preoccupied in their war for territory, El Simba plans to establish itself as a viable and feared player in this criminal game.

That is until El Simba met our hero Courage, Tuma, her faithful companion and enforcer, and a mysterious knight on horseback.

***

Monday, March 22, outside El Dorado

"My finger's gone. It's bleeding. The bone is sticking out. Where can I go? Somebody help me," Caleb screamed to himself as he ran, staggered and fell in the dusty courtyard of El Simba. Bleary-eyed and bleary-brained, he came on the desperate idea of calling on the Old Man for help- the same old man who had once broken and reassembled the young man's shoulder and pride.

Caleb knocked on the door to the old couple's room to man's voice saying, "It's open. Come in."

"What happened?" the old Man asked. "Did you cut your finger on a power tool? An axe? A sledgehammer? A saw?

Let me see it. It's a mess. The bone is shattered and needs to be smoothed before it can be stitched up to really heal. Hold on tight, I'm going to clean the wound and bandage it. This is only a stopgap measure. We'll need to take you to a doctor before it gets seriously infected. I don't have the tools to finish the job. First aid is all we do here."

The old man patched up Caleb and told him to stay out of trouble, "Go wash the truck or dig a hole. Just stay away from your uncle and Jorge," he advised the young man. Caleb never told the old man how he lost his finger, and the old man never asked.

***

Early on after their capture, Dad and Mom had made a decision to cooperate with their captures. It's been termed the Stockholm syndrome – a situation where hostages become a part of the community of hostage takers. Dad and Mom entered this situation rationally: Yes, they understood that these people had taken them against their will and might at any time torture and murder them. However, what else could they do to pass and buy some time? They would cooperate with their captures; to try and escape would be suicide.

Mom took over El Simba's housekeeping duties: She cooked for Antonio's family – Priscilla and son Juanito – plus Stefano, Antonio's mentally problematic brother, the silent Jorge, acknowledged as Antonio's enforcer and about six well armed goons who seemed to come and go and not say much. An experienced cleaning lady, she also cleaned up whenever she could. Dad ran a rudimentary aid station and helped Juanito with his English and math homework.

During the day and early into the evening, Dad and Mom could busy their fears away but at night – the fear, depression and worry about their imprisonment and possible deaths would come crashing back, wake them and introduce a harsh reality to what was supposed to have been a family vacation.

An old man, Dad knew that death was always on his shoulder. It wasn't supposed to be this way: He was to age, spoiled and respected in a modest house by the sea surrounded by blond blue eyed grandchildren; not in a narco fortress in the middle of nowhere Sinaloa. In those early morning horrors when he lay awake, he would take some solace in the Anglican prayer of humble access and repeat to himself: "Come unto me all yea that travail and are heavily laden and I will refresh you." What a beautiful word "travail" - so much better than its many circumlocutions. He loved his wife. And never blamed her for the mess they were in. He'd return to sleep exhausted in about two hours.

Mom worried. She always worried. She would wake concerned that her husband's medication was lost somewhere; and worry that they both of them would be murdered unloved and forgotten in a dirty fortress by a band of unseeing, unfeeling narco goons. She missed her children and her grandchildren. Most of all, her heart would break at the thought that her husband would suffer and die because of her family – he didn't have much – maybe that wasn't such a bad idea. Look what family had done. Her husband would tease her about her curly hair or her English because she never seemed to pronounce Tuesday and Thursday correctly– but never about the situation she had caused. She almost wished he would. It would give her a reality – a release from her guilt.

She wept because they would never have children. She cried herself to sleep with a recitation of the rosary.

Having proven their worth to the community, Mom and Dad were freed from their duct tape bonds and rewarded with freedom of movement and reasonably pleasant accommodations. They even had a plant: A cactus that seemed to watch their every move. The old couple agreed that in their difficult situation and without their beloved dog Courage, the cactus had become a pet. They also noticed that their cactus was sporting a beautiful flower and a bud – perhaps they would become grandparents to a baby cactus. In the meantime, however, Mom's biggest problem was a shrinking supply of beans –there just never seemed to be enough beans to go around. Dad agreed - adding that, while the beans seemed to disappear, their odor lingered on.

***

And yes, there were times when they remembered that they were married. Was it a tingle, a memory or hormones: Yes, they remained lovers –not with the killer passion of teenagers but lovers all the same. Even in the heart of the narco traficante's darkness.

Now, overhear the following conversation:

She: We shouldn't.
He: We should.
They: Let's. Should be fun.
She: Now stop the narco swagger. You're an old man. A respectable retired schoolteacher.

He: Come here mujer. Danger turns me on. And so do Mexican cleaning ladies.

They: Giggle.

She: You know they could kill us at any time.

He: Then we'd better hurry up.

She: Corazon...mi Corazon

He: Que tu quieres?

She: Tu. I love your blue eyes.

He: Look what you've done. I think something is going to come between us. Something big.

She: Dirty old man.

He: Yo prefero Hombre Macho.

She: It turns me on when you speak Spanish.

He: Mi Caramia.

She: Now Gomez, are we the Adams family?

He: Well, Morticia there are similarities.

She: There's something about that cactus.

He: It looks like it doesn't approve of our lovemaking. I think I'll call it Lurch.

She: Is it male or female?

He: I don't know. If it's anything like the one we've got at home, I think it reproduces by budding.

She: That doesn't sound half as much fun as making love.

He: I guess you'd have to ask the cactus.

Cactus (The Jeden):   Human lovemaking grosses me out.

She: It's like the kids. I'm not sure if they either don't approve of our love making love or don't believe we still can.

Cactus: (The Jeden):   Oh, I believe you can. I just wish you wouldn't.

He: Take those Victoria Secret panties off. They're made to be taken off –very slowly."

She: OK, I'll take them off.

He: Now, carefully place them over our disapproving prudish cactus. Look. They fit just right.

Cactus: (The Jeden): Those panties make it hard breathing. I can still hear, but at least I don't have to watch.

She: At home, we sleep or make love under a giant picture of Lupita Virgin. She blesses us. Here it's different. There's just something about that damned cactus.

They: Well, Lurch can just deal with it.

More giggles followed...then a well-pleased groan and a muffled cry of delight.

***

"At least that's over now," the Jeden thought. "They're finally finished. I'll cut the other mammals some slack on their reproduction rituals based on mating season. But humans? They seem to do it for fun. I hope she remembers to take her underpants off my bud- people around here think they're weird enough. In this awful place, even weirdness can get you killed."

"They're asleep now, so I can go invisible." The Jeden continued with his interior dialogue. "Visibility and projecting an image is hard work and a lot harder, the bigger the image. Projecting cactus is easier than Border Patrol or Fish and Game Officers and a lot easier than lions and coyotes."

The Jeden continued: "But what am I? Or to quote Jesus, one of my heroes, who said, "Who do people say that I am." It's a question that all us thinking beings should debate from time to time."

"Thinking back on the last few weeks, I remember telling Courage that I was "a kind of angel," and then Tuma repeated that idea to Cerberus. "A Kind of angel" says it best – not the kind of angel that kills the first- born or scares the bejesus out of a bunch of shepherds – that's a real angel. But a kind of angel."

"I don't really do anything," the Jeden continued. "All I can do is perceive what individuals fear and then fulfill that fear with an image. With Courage, I started with a fierce coyote – with Tuma it was a mountain lion –those images first frightened the dogs and then made them realize that as tough and smart as they were they needed some help, some guidance."

"And that's where, Officer Ariel Rabinowitz, variously of the Border Patrol and Fish and Game, made his appearance. My illumination was to be their guide – something bigger, smarter and far more powerful than they were."

"Reality?" No, not reality as such, but an image of reality that gives a framework to their goals – a working hypothesis that informs their lives."

"Funny... dogs seem to have a better grasp of what I'm up to than humans. With all their cerebral capabilities and magnificent machines, humans just see what appears to be: When they see a cactus, all they see is a cactus. When they encounter Officer Rabinowitz, all they see if Officer Rabinowitz."

"Dogs know that there is something more to reality than just what they can see with their six senses- they can see a "kind of angel." Old people too. Perhaps because their perceptions evolve as they travel to the end of their lives and toward a different dimension of what is real."

"While travelling on The Beast, I prophesized to Courage of the immediacy of hell in El Dorado. It will be soon. My illumination will be powerful, drawn from the classics and to save valuable lives. This time I will not be helping good guys as much as fighting bad guys."

***

Wednesday, March 24. El Dorado

"OK, what do we do now," I thought as we left our ride at the El Dorado bus station. "It was almost a week on various Beasts since we had left Mexicali and still no word of Mom and Dad. Were they still alive? Had they escaped? Could they be back in Indio?"

Tuma was beginning to wonder why he'd ever followed me on this very strange adventure. I wasn't so sure myself that this whole thing had been a good idea."

There seemed to be some consensus between our humans, Jesus and Juan Diego, that all they really wanted was to get some gainful employment. As if as an answer to their prayers, a young man appeared out of the smoke of the bus station and said "El Simba's looking for some soldiers."

While he looked over at Jesus and Juan Diego, they looked back at him with some wonderment in their eyes and replied, "We sure can use some work, but we've already completed our national service.

"This is a different kind of army... kind of like a market economy," the recruiter said. "They're looking for some people to work at El Simba. It's a startup located in the countryside about 10 miles from here. I can take you there."

We all got in the back of the man's pickup truck – a white, well-used Toyota – and began the bumpy ride out of town through the cornfields and to El Simba- what ever that was. The man stopped and told us that we were about a mile from the facility. "This is a far as I go," he said, dropped us off and went back to town.

We walked down the road that ran through the middle of a cornfield, and after about half a mile we saw what looked like a graveyard off to our right. Tuma and I ran ahead –as we always do –then ran back to our slow moving humans.

On one of reconnaissance missions, we saw what looked like a fort – a group of buildings constructed out of gray poured cement with walls about a meter high topped by concertina wire connecting four gray cement two story houses. The whole complex formed what looked like a square. There were no entrances. The road stopped at a massive wood and steel reinforced door big enough for a car to enter. I could see humans with guns walking behind the walls.

Tuma and I ran up to the door to see if we could get in and check out what this El Simba was all about. "These people couldn't be that bad," I thought - even though they had all that scary armament which was much superior to the small arms employed by the Mexican army – because they had…a doggy door. Yes, a doggy door right in the middle of that giant door. Bad people don't like dogs," I thought. "Not necessarily." I learned later.

***

Heading straight for the doggy door, Tuma and I crashed though it making the same sound as the one at home – wiky... wiky...wiky... However, at the beginning of what appeared to be kind of a courtyard, we didn't meet Mom and Dad, but we met Cerberus a sixty-pound Pit Bull ferocious in a body of bone and hide stretched tightly over powerful muscles. His eyes were slits in a head of pure jawbone and teeth. His ears were little more than nubs.

"What are you hairy weaklings doing here," Cerberus growled at Tuma and me. "I am THE DOG and no other dogs are welcome. I'm so mean...so ferocious ...that they named me after the three-headed dog of Greek mythology. Get out of here now or face the consequences."

In my most diplomatic manner, I quietly barked that we were not there to dispute his territory but to find my humans who were being held captives somewhere near El Dorado. While I was barking, Tuma moved closer to Cerberus. I backed away.

"Hey, get off my case, wolf dog," Cerberus snarled at Tuma. Tuma backed away and I moved closer.

"Look you little so and so," he snarled at me. "I don't like being crowded." I backed away and Tuma moved closer.

With Tuma closing in, I tore into Cerberus and bit his ear tearing a little bit of his flesh and blood in my effort. Just like I did back in the Sunnyvale Doggie Park.

Cerberus was livid and came after me, snarling in a most uncivil manner. Just about to lock his jaws on my hip, he stopped. Tuma was holding our host's neck in his 120 pounds of wolf teeth and fury.

Cerberus gave up. Tail between his legs and belly first on the ground. "You guys think with one mind," he whimpered, "one of you is Lightening the other is Thunder.

"No," I barked back, "my name is Courage but my new humans call me Lobita while my big friend here is Tuma but goes by the name of Lobo. But now, let me give you a short lesson in evolution:"

"Your breed is about 500 years old. Bred to fight – quite literally in a pit with a bull (I'd hate to be that bull). You are strong, brave and can take incredible amounts of punishment."

"On the other hand," I barked, "Tuma and I are one step from our common wolf ancestors. You are a fighter, but we are killers. We cooperate as a pack, and as you can see, we think with almost one mind when taking down prey. You can sustain injuries. We can't. One serious injury and we're dinner. If circumstances were different, we would have eaten you."

"Glad you didn't," Cerberus whimpered back.

In barks so low, I could hardly hear their conversation, Cerberus remarked to Tuma that I was a beautiful dog and asked if Tuma and I were boyfriend and girlfriend. Tuma replied that, no we weren't, but that we were friends – a bond greater than mere lovers. He went on to confide to Cerberus that he was... well, that way.

"Do you keep a nice doghouse? Dig beautiful holes?" Cerberus returned. "Did you ever, what do they call it? Cruise?"

"Well, on my way down here, I had a few encounters – got myself a terrible case of fleas for my efforts," Tuma confessed. "That is until I hooked up with Courage –she's very strict about that sort of thing so I cleaned up my act. Yes, now there was an incident outside of Brawley – she caught me with a new friend – chewed me out ...snarled at my behavior...she was on my case for a week. Nothing since then. I don't want to risk her anger."

"The rest," Tuma replied, "I'm just a regular male dog. Well, sometimes I get cranky when Courage presses me for a commitment I just can't make. Yes, I have had some problems relating to other dogs in the doggy park."

"I lived in a Sunnyvale apartment with my two fathers," Tuma continued –"that was where I met Courage. Then my fathers moved to the forest outside of Santa Cruz. I just loved it there– the smells, the hunting – nothing like taking down a squirrel. The taste still lingers in my mouth. Then my fathers separated and I ended up alone. I didn't know what to do until the Jeden hooked me back up with Courage. The rest is history."

"What's a Jeden," Cerberus asked.

Tuma did his best to explain. "You see a Jeden is neither a plant nor an animal – male or female- and can take any form – coyote, mountain lion, Border Patrol or Train conductor. The Jeden is kind of an angel and appears when you need...a "Jeden."

"Now back to Courage," Cerberus questioned softly. "Do you think that maybe she would like to party."

Tuma warned Cerberus that I treasured my virtue, and, if he made any untoward moves in my direction he'd be lucky if all he lost was an ear. Cerberus backed off.

"OK, boys," I barked at those two, "enough guy talk. We have work to do. We've already wasted a day getting here. Now let's get to work. We have a mission."

***

Just as we had established our all important hierarchical canine structures and Tuma and Cerberus bonded, a slack jawed young man – fair skinned, about five eight- approached

Cerberus and addressed him in what I could only see as a very rude manner.

"Hey Burro, yea that's you Cerberus," he said to our new friend. "Why don't you fight the big one –yea, the one that looks like a wolf?"

Cerberus declined to fight and remained submissive.

"I'm talking to you. Fight or it's the club," the man yelled at the pit bull. He then raised the club to strike at Cerberus. Looked like he'd done it before.

"That was enough," Tuma and I agreed silently. We crowded the man, showed the teeth and snarled in unison. "Cerberus is one of us now," to this unwelcome and unpleasant human.

The man left muttering something about dogs and revenge.

"Do you know who that was," Cerberus barked. "That was Stefano, brother of El Patron Antonio. He's very brave when others are weak. He loses it when confronted with strength… the stupid clown face."

At this point, I was dusty, hungry and thirsty. I asked Cerberus if there was any water or food or anything in this awful place to calm my aching tummy.

"Oh yes there is," Cerberus replied. "There are two humans who were kidnapped and dragged here all tied up and gagged but now live in a small room in the second house on your left…About 100 yards from here. They put out water and food for me. I really like them."

"An old white man and a middle aged Mexican lady?" I questioned our new friend.

"Yes," he replied. "They're almost part of the community now. They help out a lot with things like, cooking, healing and teaching – things that Antonio's goons can't or won't do."

My humans. My humans are here. Alive and in danger but here and so far unharmed. I don't believe it; my quest is almost at an end. I could hardly contain myself.

My tail was wagging so hard I was afraid I'd break my back. I jumped...ran and then jumped again. I did 100 yards in under 5 seconds nosed their door open...saw Dad and Mom ...I climbed in his lap and then snuggled with her. I was so happy...

I peed...

All over both of them and the floor and a little bit even on the furniture. You know what, they didn't seem to mind at all. They snuggled me and cooed right back – in fact, if truth be told, my humans may also have peed- a profound pee of joy. Tuma watched the whole scene and reminded us that joyful peeing was not what we were here to do – our work was just ahead of us and we'd better get on with it.

***

"Where are the dogs," Juan Diego asked Jesus as evening deepened and the air chilled. "They just seemed to have disappeared into that fort or whatever it is. Sure is ugly –all gray ... no trees ...no flowers ... not even any grass."

"Yes," agreed Jesus, "the people in that little "fort" seemed to have cleared, what I remember from my army training, as a field of fire. There's nothing within 100 yards of the place. The corn has been cut down and it looks like some grave stones have been moved away. See the guys behind the wall? They don't look like any soldiers I knew during my service."

"That place is creepy and scary," Juan Diego replied. "But we must "soldier on" and see if they have any paying work that we can do."

"Or want to do," Jesus concluded.

Approaching the complex, Jesus and Juan Diego noticed doors within doors: There was the main door – large enough for a car, then a smaller door within the main door which appeared to be for humans and a doggy door within that. All were heavy black painted wood – reinforced with armored steel bands. The rest of the complex was reinforced poured concrete – even the roofs of the buildings – and impervious to small arms fire.

"It would take an army tank or heavy artillery to break through that portal," Juan Diego observed.

"I think that's the purpose," Jesus agreed. "It looks like they would take unkindly to unwanted visitors."

The guards looked down at Jesus and Juan Diego with rifles cocked and pointed at them.

"What do we do now," Juan Diego asked.

"Knock on the door," Jesus replied. "What else can we do? We're here now, and can't go back; if they want to shoot us, there's very little we can do about it."

They knocked. The door opened to an unarmed teenaged boy with a crudely bandaged hand. "Pat him down," one of the guards told the boy. He checked the men for arms and found none. He was accompanied by a fierce pit bull.

"What do you want?" one of the guards asked.

"Work," they replied in unison.

"OK, let them in Caleb," the guard said. "El Patron is not here right now and won't be here until tomorrow, so take them in to see his wife Priscilla. She should know what to do with them. Third building. Second floor. First door on the left. While you're at it, Caleb we'll check them out to see if it's really work they're looking for or just snooping around for information. If they are looking for information, we'll have to assure El Patron that they don't talk. He doesn't take kindly to spies."

***

Caleb escorted Jesus and Juan Diego to the office shared by Antonio and his wife Priscilla. He managed the operation; she took care of the books. If that's what she really did.

Priscilla's side of the office was a manager's nightmare: Papers strewn all over the place and an ash tray overflowing with cigarettes- smoked down to the filter tip. When they came in, she was talking on her cell with her mother. It took a while for her to realize that Juan Diego and Jesus were even there. Her voice was husky and her breath smelled of smoke. Her face was acne scarred and lined with high times and a lot of dope. She was 25 years old.

Drinking a diet coke, she affected a tight short skirt, a plunging neckline that showed her chest to its best advantage and mucho bling- gold rings, a diamond broach and some very expensive dangly jewelry thingies. Her husband Antonio couldn't resist her high heals and fishnet stockings. Similar to her Mom, she was long on makeup and short on deodorant. The best perfume money could buy didn't mask what she referred to as her "European" odor. She'd never star in a Mexican novella.

The last thing in the world Priscilla wanted to do was interview and hire some new thugs for Antonio's empire. She motioned the two to a couple of plastic chairs and told them to wait. She told them that El Patron would be back in a while, but she wasn't sure when.

"Why do I stay?" Priscilla asked herself. "This place is boring and those thugs – los goonos-mundos. They all look the same. Short stocky, covered with tattoos – a lot of 13s – I can't tell them apart. Plus they're downright creepy. El Dorado has no club life and the closest Starbucks is all the way to Culiacan."

"Are flowers too much to ask? Or maybe a few palm trees? – No I get well-manicured dust. A "house" in the country surrounded by empty fields and concertina wire-miles from nowhere and with uniformed people sneaking around in the graveyard – it's a race to death between the Mexican Marines and Los Zetas or the Sinaloa Cartel."

"It was fun at first," Priscilla continued her musings. "Antonio is gorgeous – maybe short - but he's agile as a cat and looks like an Aztec prince. Straight arrow though and always dressed in black like a priest. I remember when my girlfriends and I took off from fun in Mazatlan to the wilds of Sinaloa. The cartel, the cocaine and the violence were real turn-ons. He was cute and very protective and gave me the best coca. I was stoned and couldn't resist him; or was it that he couldn't resist me. Latino men can't get enough of us tall blue-eyed blondes. And this blue-eyed tall blond loves the danger …the brutality and the blood.

"But I'm bored," she concluded. "The bling is great and I love the Escalade. The kid – our beloved child – Juanito is pretty much Antonio's responsibility. As is his "Retard" brother Stefano. He even named this organization El Simba because his brother liked the movie, *The Lion King*. Didn't he know, that lions make horrible fathers?"

"I hate the weather –hot and dry in the spring – hot and muggy in the summer with clouds of mosquitos and thunder storms. Palm Springs was better –hot as Hades in the summer – but at least you knew where you stood."

Priscilla had met a new guy- her Sancho, her lover at one of the clubs. Skip was a handsome, rich and white guy who lived in one of those fancy gated Palm Springs communities. "He's married to some gringa bitch (Gringa is a perjoritive term for an American woman.) but aren't all the good ones?" she said to herself.

Priscilla was Sycorax' love child. She'd tell her daughter stories of her father a handsome, wealthy and tall Spanish man who would have married her if he hadn't met with a tragic accident. Her brother Caleb was a mistake- a combo of lust, desperation and alcohol.

"I married Antonio, a thug who should have been a priest," Priscilla realized. "When Mom comes, I'm out of here."

***

Thursday, March 25

"I'm a seminary educated thug who should have been a priest," Antonio thought to himself as he walked into the office early next morning. The violence was getting to him.

"Where have you been," Priscilla asked.

"From walking up and down on the earth," he answered.

"What does that mean?" she asked.

"Oh it's something from the Bible – the Book of Job. It's what Satan says to God when asked what he was up to," Antonio replied.

"Just in a day's work." Antonio continued. "Jorge and I went to town to remind a bar owner and one of our ladies to mind their manners. They're the ones who ripped off Caleb. We exacted discipline – no lasting damage: just a knee to the groin…a few punches in the stomach… and some missing teeth. He'll recover and his dentist will cheer our efforts; I told the lady's pimp that she had best not rob one of our own. He'll take care of her. Caleb may be stupid, ugly and deformed, but he's one of us. We got the money back… plus interest."

"I just picked up Juanito at school," he continued. "Dropped him off with the old man to study English and math. The child is falling behind in his studies…living here is a tough environment for a youngster."

Antonio looked around to see two job seekers still sitting on those green plastic chairs: A tall white man, bearded and gone to fat and a shorter, dark complected man on the thin side. They both appeared to be in their mid twenties. They'd been there all night. Must have slept sitting up. Probably very hungry.

"What brings you two to our lovely country estate," Antonio asked the two exhausted petitioners darkly.

Both of them responded with one-word "work."

"Do you know how to handle weapons," he asked.

"We have both completed our military service," they responded.

"I was awarded a marksmanship medal in boot camp for my success on the firing range," Juan Diego added.

"What kind of weapon did you qualify on," Antonio asked.

"An M-14," Juan Diego answered.

Antonio noted: "We haven't used those in years, but I guess that's the best the Mexican army can get. It'll do the trick but the clip is small and rapid fire is not so good as with more modern rifles. We chose the AK 47 over the M-16. It's just as accurate but not as subject to malfunction like its American cousin. We hope to get the new Bushmaster – you know, the assault weapon that made such an impression in Sandy Hook."

"Our handguns are pretty much a matter of choice – I have a Walther, Jorge prefers his Glock – Stefano loves his American Colt 44 – got it off a dead Mexican soldier. Makes a terrible racket when fired, but Baby Brother loves the drama. As a rule, unless we can recycle our weapon of choice, we get the best arms our Cousin to the North can offer. The U.S. isn't all hung up with gun control like Mexico. We get our guns from a nice little gun shop in Texas –same outfit that gave the crazy major at Fort Hood his fire sticks."

"But, with Mexican gun laws so strict, how do you get all these fancy weapons," Juan Diego asked.

"Oh, my naive friend, "Antonio replied, "money, influence and threats can buy anything including the Mexican border guards."

But how about the Americans who bring guns into Mexico and get caught, they end up in jail – not a particularly nice place –and spend a lot of money and time getting out," Jesus chimed in.

"How often can I repeat it – money, influence and threats," Antonio replied. "When the old gringo tries to bring his weapon through Mexican customs, he gets caught and always fails to possess the wherewithal to keep from getting sent to jail. We narcos have people crossing the border all the time – only 1% out of 99% of border crossers are bad – and the bad guys bring in the arms to Mexico. We have a special gun store in Texas. With US gun laws weak to non-existent, it's easy to buy legally or purchase from someone who is legal but who will sell you his weapon for a profit. You can also contact any number of crooks who front the millions of guns stolen yearly from Americans who think that they are protecting their home and family.

"And you?" Antonio addressed Jesus. "What do you say to weaponry? What did you qualify on when you were in the Army? What's your weapon of choice?"

"I am opposed to all violence in any form," Jesus replied. "I enjoyed conscientious objector status in the army and was neither qualified on nor ordered to carry a weapon."

"Violence is what we're all about," Antonio responded. "We'll see what we can do with you later."

Antonio called Jorge over for a brief conversation.

"We have a problem out back," Antonio said to Jorge, his lead enforcer. "Why don't you take our friend Juan Diego here with you and see how well he can handle a weapon. Take a shovel."

Jorge motioned Juan Diego to come with him. They left the office, past Caleb and Cerberus out the human door and into what had been a well-kept cemetery. The only building left was a small, gray stone monument. Juan Diego could see a very frightened young man – maybe 15 years old – manacled to a gravestone. It looked like the young man had been there a while.

They approached within three feet of the prisoner and the terror in the man's eyes burned through Juan Diego's heart.

"Take this 38, Police Special, and kill him," Jorge instructed.

"I can't do that," Juan Diego sputtered shaking all over. "I don't know him. What did he do?"

"I don't know really," Jorge returned. "He must have disobeyed El Patron. Maybe a spy. Whatever it was, Antonio wants you to kill him."

Jorge handed the gun to Juan Diego.

Juan Diego fired 5 shots all over the place except at the man.

Jorge took the gun from Juan Diego and with the remaining bullet in the chamber killed the man. One bullet execution style.

"You never killed before, right?" Jorge said to Juan Diego. "Don't worry it gets easier. You may even get to enjoy it. Bury him. Bury him well. We have a lot of coyotes around here, and they just love to dig up dead bodies. El Patron gets upset if he sees body parts littering the landscape. He's fastidious that way."

With my previous employer," Jorge continued, "we placed the body in a barrel filled with lime that destroyed all the soft tissue. The remaining bones were then thrown into a common grave – fossa clandestines - with a lot of other bones. Identity, even with most advanced forensic techniques is virtually impossible. The person who administers this task is called el pozelero after the cook of pozoles our beloved Mexican stew."

"Some of our more tenderhearted compatriots try to memorialize the gang war dead whose bones and other remains are mixed with each others," Jorge continued. "These well meaning folks – usually girl friends and mothers –take concrete slabs and put the faces and names of their sons and lovers whose remains may or may not be interred with each other. To me, the whole thing is kind of stupid, and very sad," he concluded.

"See you in an hour. Don't miss dinner. If you do, it will be your last."

Juan Diego bent over and wretched. And wretched again. As soon as he could stand up he began to dig hard; he dug fast and he dug deep but nothing – no amount of physical strain - could erase the terror that he saw in that young man's eyes before he died. Those eyes … that terror beyond fear… burned into his heart. Those eyes would flame at him every night for the rest of his life.

While Juan Diego was still digging, Jorge went back to the complex, smiled at Cerberus and gave a thumbs-up sign to Antonio who responded in kind.

***

Some people say it's the environment – others that it's a pathological condition or even an extra chromosome- but whatever it was, Jorge liked what he did. An orphan Kaibile from Guatemala drafted into Los Zetas, he became a good student and killed his first target at age 13 – another boy soldier. It was easy. It was fun. He loved to see the terror in the victim's eyes and the all powerful – Godlike taking of another life. His killings mounted, as he became El Tirito, the executioner, for the Zetas in their conflict with El Cartel de Gulfo.

As young Jorge grew in strength and brutal experience, he became a very effective torturer – the whole process right down to administering the electrodes excited him. The longer it took and the worse the pain the better. Death trumped love every time. Love for a woman came with too many encumbrances.

Word had it that he was kicked out of Los Zetas for excessive brutality. He knew the dark humor about his arrival and position; he also knew that with Los Zetas there was no such thing as excessive brutality and that nobody left Los Zetas except through death's door. He was on loan to El Simba and Antonio from Los Zetas to keep watch on this upstart outfit and, depending on the circumstances, either take it over or squash it like a bug.

Jorge kept clear of the Sinaloa cartel. That kind of competition can get you killed. Just to cover his bets, however, he kept a framed picture of Jesus Mal Verde over his bed. Who knows when a competitor might win the game, take over the territory and come calling? He'd never get a narcocorrido, a popular song singing the praises of a particular cartel boss. Nobody would sing the praises of El Sapo –The Toad- his nickname; he was too ugly for praise. That was OK with Jorge – he'd take fear over flattery any day.

Although lacking in formal education, Jorge was intelligent and quickly mastered the technology of the armaments given him and even picked up some English. His math skills were good, and he loved computer games – the more violent the better. But he could never understand Don Quixote – "what a fool," he thought after reading a few chapters, "why did the author ever spend his time writing about a crazy old man."

***

Later that evening Antonio engaged Jesus and said, "As you can see, now, what was your name –Jesus? We are a business; every business needs records. My wife, Priscilla is very good at certain things, but not very interested in record keeping. Do you know anything about office procedure? Computers?"

"Yes, in fact I do. I studied computer science at the Technological University in Monterey, but lost the business when I couldn't afford the "protection" offered by Los Zetas," Jesus replied. "If you wish, I could set up an Excel program that would organize your income – debits and credits and receivables. That sort of thing."

"Go to it," Antonio replied. "My mother in law will be visiting shortly and I'd like to have the office shipshape. Show her what a good office manager her daughter is. There's also an Internet connection. I'll have Priscilla keep the password to herself until we can be sure that you can be trusted. She's gone back to the house and is enjoying a catch-me-up cocktail or two or three before dinner."

Jesus stayed in the office most of the evening. Setting up the office computer system was the easy part: He put the papers in piles according to subject. Then he input the data in the Excel program using a simple T system of accounting-red for owed and black for received. There was a lot of red – many receivables but very little received in the black column. He'd have to talk about that with Antonio. The hard part was enduring the smells: cigarettes – well, he could throw away the buts but the tobacco stink lingered on – ditto for the cheap perfume and the European odor of his new boss's wife.

After a restless night sleep with the hostages – the floor of their room was at best uncomfortable and sharing it with Juan Diego was noisy and snore-ridden – Jesus went back to the office. Using Excel, he'd cleared up their accounts. Now he was bored and went looking for more places to play. Without the password he was limited, but he was able to attach a printer that was just kind of lying around and write a report: First he tried a pie chart and then a bar graph – he liked the pie chart better and printed it out. Word was easy to access so he wrote up an accompanying report. Then he put it together for Antonio, who like Jesus was an early riser and had just returned to the office from taking his son to school.

At heart a hacker, Jesus couldn't stop with pleasing his boss and just had to find where he could go with his newfound toy. "Password? "What's the password? No going any further without the password," he thought. He could see that Priscilla used the computer for e-mail and probably had a Facebook account. But she didn't like or have any interest in computers. People like that usually had very simple passwords. He tried 1,2,3,4 ...no luck. Then "password." That worked.

Jesus had just opened a new world of knowledge and communication. It would cost him his life.

***

Friday, March 26

Early next morning, Jesus had hacked into Priscilla's E-Mail account. "Oh, Bad Girl,' he thought. "So, she' got a guy in Palm Springs – practically next door to her Mom – oh my God –her Mom is Sycorax. The awful woman we met at the border. Said she see us again. Hated me. Remember me, she said "Sycorax" when she steamed off in that black Continental to visit her son – must be Caleb – in Mexico. And she's visiting soon. Better be careful...keep a low profile...and find out what's going on."

Jesus' curiosity got the better of him and let his fingers do some walking –"don't try the El Dorado police – they'll be in somebody's pocket," he thought...now try Wikipedia ...no luck ...they'll just have some pap on the cartels that everybody knows. They don't have anything on El Simba at all. Maybe I should try...what's that American group...yea, that's the FBI... see if they know anything."

"Bingo. They are currently investigating El Simba to see if they are holding two American hostages for ransom–an old white man and middle aged Mexican woman. Agent in charge: Malcolm Macduff - fluent in Spanish and specialist in hostage negotiations. He has information that an informant was recently murdered and buried in the graveyard adjacent the El Simba complex. Please contact me at 555-555-5555 or mduff@fbi.gov if you have any further information. Your identity will remain confidential. There is a reward of $100, 000 for information leading to a successful conclusion of this case. "

"That must be why Juan Diego looked so ashen last night – looked sick – didn't eat much" Jesus thought. "And the snoring – yes, there were cries from his sleep like "don't"... "don't make me"... "I'm not a killer"...

Jesus hoped that Juan Diego hadn't killed that guy. Probably that awful Jorge or some other thug did it. Juan Diego was out in the courtyard planting some palms and what looked like flowers. Must be prepping for a visit from Sycorax, La Suegra – Antonio's, El Patron's much -feared mother-in-law.

***

Late next morning, Sycorax made her entrance. Stealth was not her long suite. Her car was big, black and noisy. Exhaust and dust tailed it as it came up the dirt road. La Suegra (the mother-in-law) was big, 5'10" and approaching 200 pounds, white and noisy – profanity exploded between tugs on her forever cigarette and her deodorant failed again. Her mascara dripped down her face like rain after a thunderstorm.

"Open the door you idiot," she screamed at Juan Diego who happened to have the misfortune to be planting trees near the front of the complex. The horn blared and didn't stop blaring until she and the car screeched to a dusty stop outside the family living quarters. Tuma and I disliked the noise and rudeness of that woman so we crowded her.

"I want to see my beautiful daughter …my only child and get those stupid looking dogs out of my face," she hooted as she blasted open the door and threw herself into the office.

I remembered her and became very worried. She hated Jesus, and I was at a loss at what to do. I could show her the teeth, but that didn't seem to be the thing to do right now.

Tuma and I also noticed something wrong with Juan Diego – he was drinking more, not eating and looking very pale. Where's a Jeden when I need one. The Jeden told me that things were going to be bad outside El Dorado– but he didn't tell me what to do. I was so happy to see Mom and Dad that I forgot to take care of business.

***

Prior to Sycorax noisy arrival, Antonio had very wisely excused Jesus from the office with instructions to go help Juan

Diego with the yard work. He roused his wife Priscilla from bed and helped her into her newly clean and orderly office. He congratulated himself on the work Jesus had done. *She can brag on this now, and I can keep that awful woman, her Mom and my mother in law, off my back for a while.* He left the office.

"Oh, what a beautiful office you have my dear," Sycorax gushed to her daughter. "Everything is orderly and clean. Access your E-Mail. We're alone together. Does old Montezuma, your legally wedded husband, know about Skip? I hope not. You never know what these Mexican narcos might do if they got jealous."

"Let's look. Wow, that's pretty passionate stuff you've written. Yes, his wife just doesn't understand him. Too bad… So often the case. They wouldn't stray if wifypoo were better at what she was supposed to do. And what's this," she continued. The FBI? Agent MacDuff is investigating El Simba. He's right here in El Dorado and speaks fluent Spanish. Did you contact him? If not, I think Antonio would be very interested in finding and silencing the spy in our midst."

"It wasn't me," Priscilla replied. "I'll bet it was that awful Jesus. He spent a lot of time here last night."

***

"Oh my baby, my youngest, my baby boy, what have they done to you? Your finger. It looks awful. It must be infected. You absolutely must see a doctor …and I mean right now," Sycorax exclaimed to all who could hear and many who didn't want to. Caleb bent over with a cramp and feared the pinches.

"OK Sycorax," Antonio replied. "We'll send Caleb to a good doctor in El Dorado tomorrow."

"Caleb," he continued. "Have you mastered the art of driving standard transmission yet? Is that a yes? If so, take the truck. I don't have anybody free to drive you there right now. My amigos are either working the grounds, disciplining our clients or serving guard duty. No funny business this time. I've got people on the lookout for you. Don't mess up. Or it will be more than a finger this time."

"Can I take the dogs?" Caleb asked.

"OK with the two new ones – their names? Oh yes, Lobo and Lobita. You'll have to leave Cerberus here. We need him at the gate. You'll need to stay the night so here's the address of the doctor and a safe house. I'll be watching. See you in the morning – before noon."

Caleb, Tuma and I returned back as scheduled.

***

* Please note that until now the text has been written in the first person dog. I was really there. Dogs are like that. Nobody notices us, but we notice everything and hear and smell more. However, during the events surrounding Antonio's and Jesus' death, Tuma, Caleb and I were in in El Dorado and away from the El Simba complex and not able to eyewitnesses what actually took place. Therefore, in order to complete my narrative, I have had to rely on secondary sources including Agent MacDuff's FBI report and Juan Diego's personal diary. My analysis is based on my interpretative and intuitive understanding of the persons and environment directly involved in the events of that fateful late afternoon and evening. Any errors are mine and mine only.

***

Saturday, March 27

"Oh, Antonio," Sycorax crackled to her son in law out of a cloud of cigarette smoke. "Do you know a Malcolm MacDuff?"

Antonio thought for a while ... "yes, I remember him from when I was in the seminary. We had long and impassioned theological discussions that seemed to last all night. He's what they call a Mormon and was in Mexico doing his missionary requirement. I could never understand his religion or his commitment to it. However, our conversations were usually enjoyable. There were never any hard feelings, and his Spanish was perfect."

"You know, it's funny," Antonio continued. "I could have sworn I saw him downtown El Dorado having a soft drink. Hasn't changed much. But I didn't get a chance to see if it was really he. If it was, what was he doing here?"

"If you haven't guessed by now," Sycorax continued. "He's now Special Agent Malcolm MacDuff, FBI, and he's investigating you and El Simba."

"Me? How'd you find that out? Why didn't I know," Antonio reacted in alarm.

"Well it seemed that your new soldier Jesus - computer expert and conscientious objector - was doing a little research on his own," she continued snuffing out her cigarette. "Your boy wonder cracked Priscilla's password and let his fingers do the walking. Jesus and Agent MacDuff now know a lot more about you and your operation than they did two days ago."

She did not tell Antonio that Jesus also knew of Pricilla's American lover.

By now it was early evening and Antonio paled. Then called over to Jorge who seemed to appear out of nowhere. He gave his enforcer the following instructions:

"Tell our new gardeners –Jesus and Juan Diego -that they have another task. Bring their shovels. We have had a death in the family and need to prepare his grave. Take Stefano and the other Jorge with you.

***

Jorge and the other Jorge picked up Antonio's brother Stefano as they walked over to Jesus and Juan Diego who were hard at work. They were doing their best with the meager resources at hand to add some beauty – well, maybe not beauty – but at least to plant some palms and flowers in order to soften the hard edges of the compound and please Antonio's mother in law.

As they left the compound, Jesus couldn't help noticing that both Jorge's and Stefano were heavily armed. Juan Diego noticed the guns as well but, remembering his first execution, made no comments to his friend.

"Dig it, long; dig it wide; and dig it deep. We have a big body to bury here." Jorge instructed the two. And, indeed they did.

Jorge then nodded to Stefano and the other Jorge. The two then knocked Jesus to the ground and tied him up with duck tape. He was a big man but gone to soft, totally unprepared and offered little resistance.

"Can I kill him…can I …can I," Stefano cried to Jorge who nodded his approval.

Stefano leveled his Colt 44 at Jesus and with a crash of thunder – blood, bones and screams of pain – missed the executioner's mark as his shot tore into Jesus's shoulder.

Jorge motioned Stefano to stand back. He placed his Glock to the back of Jesus' head and let loose two shots – pflunk...pflunk as the silenced bullet left the weapon, crashed through the victims skull and entered his medulla. Jesus died instantly.

"I want his shoes. They're Timberlines." Stefano demanded.

Jorge agreed to Stefano's request but reminded him that they needed to get back to the safety of the compound because Mexican Marines might infiltrate the area. He then told Juan Diego to bury the body.

"Why did you kill him," Juan Diego wept. "He never did anything. He didn't believe in violence."

"Boss's orders. Do you want to join him? There's loads of room in this graveyard. I'm positive we can find some other gravediggers. Plus Stefano could use some practice," Jorge laughed.

Juan Diego declined and began to bury his friend.

The others left the cemetery to join Antonio, his wife, mother in law and some other soldiers for dinner of Mom's finest pozole. Most laughed over Stefano's near miss; Priscilla was stoned and Sycorax polished off three martinis. Antonio ate stone-faced. Mom and Dad made excuses and ate by themselves.

**

"Why do you weep, Juan Diego?" a sweet female voice sounded in his head as he did his best to fill in Jesus' grave. The others had left to celebrate another brutality...Jesus's murder ...just another insignificant innocent death in the Mexican drug war.

"I weep because I betrayed my friend," Juan Diego countered the voice. "I did nothing to save him. He died without a priest, without last rights or extreme unction. Now I don't have the strength to bury him – they pushed him in the grave face up. His eyes stare through me – I can't cover them but I must. If not, the coyotes would devour his body and spread his bones all over Sinaloa."

"Look in your pockets my child," the voice continued.

"I have no coins to cover his eyes," Juan Diego responded.

"Look in your pockets. Take the coins and cover his eyes," the voice urged Juan Diego.

Juan Diego found two pesos in his pockets – "assuredly they weren't there before," he thought. Then he bent over the grave and closed Jesus' eyes with the coins. Upon arising from the grave, he saw:

Lupita Virgin. Shining in her glory. And his eyes cleared.

"You must now bury your friend in the proper way," she commanded.

"But, Holy Mother, I am a poor ignorant farmer. My priest called me "burro" because I had neither the time nor the education to master the catechism. I can't perform the holy offices."

"Yes you can – *si tu puede*, you have the gift my child. Now begin," Lupita Virgin continued. "Your tears will serve as the most blest holy water."

Juan Diego surprised himself. In dignity, he repeated extreme unction and the rosary as well.

"Your friend Jesus is in a better place now," Lupita Virgin reminded Juan Diego. "You will always sadden when you think of his murder. But try to remember his life and the divinity of friendship. As our Lord said, "there is no greater virtue than to give your life for your friends."

"Juan Diego, my child, I will stay with you in spirit. I have always been with you although you never knew it – mine was the cool cloth on your forehead when you had fever …mine was the comfort you took when your classmates teased you about your old clothes…mine was the peace you found when there was nothing else…"

"Before I leave, Juan Diego, you must promise me one thing: Stop killing yourself," she added.

"I may be ignorant of theology but I know suicide is a mortal sin. I would never kill myself," he replied.

"Every drink you take kills you," she said.

With those words echoing in his ears, Juan Diego threw his flask in the grave with Jesus and buried both.

"If you will, Holy Mother," Juan Diego asked. "I have a question. I know that vengeance is the Lord's responsibility, but my friend's murderer must be brought to justice. What should I do?"

"Your question can not be answered. Antonio was Jesus' murderer and the thug Jorge and the crazed Stefano killed your friend. Antonio was a good man, but our holy mother church failed him. A sinful priest mad with lust forced him out of a holy ministry and into a life of crime. He then succumbed to the sin of ambition and pride. He has murdered many but killed no one."

Lupita Virgin then left Juan Diego to his own devices: He would never drink again. He would now play the fool, gain the trust of the narcos and, when the time came, even the score with his friend's murderer.

CHAPTER 6

THE CACTUS SMILED: PART 2

Life's time can proceed without beginning or end, tediously wandering from day to day, from month to month and year to year. Then life happens in a day, a minute, and a second.

WEDNESDAY, MARCH 31, 2010.

Something was wrong. Dreadfully wrong. Dogs know: It's probably a combination of our superior senses of smell, hearing or 100,000 years of evolution, but dogs know. Intuitively we know far more and far quicker than humans. We know so much about them; they know so little about us.

The trip to El Dorado was fun. After the doctor repaired his wound, Caleb loosened up a bit and found that the company of dogs beats that of humans every time. We really wanted to take Cerberus that old marsh mellow -all bluff and bluster on the outside and the sweetest mush on the inside. He's also a lot of fun, and he and Caleb seemed to be developing a special relationship, but they kept our friend tied up inside the compound. I guess he was supposed to scare away intruders. Fat chance.

At first we noticed that Juan Diego seemed to have taken charge of the door to the compound, but he was different. I can't say how but different – but he acted differently and even looked different. He radiated more...much more than just having giving up the bottle.

Jesus was not to be found. Usually the two were together. While Tuma looked after Juan Diego, Jesus was my responsibility. I heard the humans laughing about killing Jesus, and I feared that I had failed in my responsibility.

There was little I could do other than follow my nose to the graveyard and sniff the ground. Yes, it was Jesus newly murdered and buried. I had failed to protect my human. Guilt was an understatement. I tried to excuse my inattention with the knowledge that Jesus would soon die of cancer and two bullets to the head were far more merciful than death by that loathsome disease. But it was false logic and no excuse. I had failed. There was no way around it.

I was devastated by the loss of Jesus and my excuse about his cancer rang hollow. Then and there I resolved to protect my humans no matter the cost. I would never to let my humans – Dad and Mom – out of sight and out of my protection.

After howling a prayer of mourning, I hurried back to the compound and my humans. When I found out that they were all right I wagged my tail hard enough to break my back. Peed a little. And dug a hole.

***

Antonio, Jorge and Priscilla were all talking about Sycorax' departure planned for early the following morning. First, she was to go to Tijuana, load up on meth and coca, then follow route 2 to the East Mexicali crossing. There she would offload the goods at a tunnel near the border crossing with the US. After she passed the border, she'd pick up the goods at the tunnel ending just east of Calexico. Then she'd take route 98 to Glamis where she'd distribute the meth to the crazed off roaders who were busy destroying the sand dunes and themselves in the hurly burly of the Imperial Valley Recreational Area. A little bit of meth can go a long way.

Sycorax would compete with the major cartels – Los Zetas, El Cartel de Gulfo, and Sinaloa and a few minor ones – who lurk around the Mexican border crossing to the United States. If one or more cartel knows of a drug movement across the border by a competitive cartel, they will notify the American border patrol that will in turn apprehend the smuggler. For example, if a member of the Sinaloa cartel is moving a cargo of meth or cocaine across the border, a member of Los Zetas would notify the border patrol of the action. The border patrol would in turn arrest the mule of the competing cartel. This process is called *Chivatazo* or "Goat Call."

There are winners in Chivatzo: The US Border Patrol can claim a big drug bust and the arrest of smuggler. Right behind the winning US agency is the competing cartel or other competing narco traficantes who have caused their competitor to lose a mule and a load of meth, marijuana or cocaine.

And there are losers in Chivatzo: The informed on cartel loses some goods –easily replaced by more drugs south of the border when street value north of the border which can exceed the original cost by four figures. The big loser is the smuggler who will either rot in an American jail or be returned to Mexico where, more often than not, he will face a sudden and brutal death at the hands of one or another narco traficantes.

Sycorax had been subject to numerous Chivatazos and often questioned by the US authorities on her frequent border crossings, but suspicious Migra had never found anything in her car or on her person. It was not the Border Patrol methods that failed, but there was good reason that they found nothing. There was simply nothing to be found because, while she was being questioned, an underground mule was moving her product under the very feet of the Border Patrol to a point close by the border crossing on the American side.

The United States part of Sycorax' journey was to be less travelled: she planned to carry the coca and meth while travelling with her daughter Priscilla ostensibly to meet her new friend Skip who lived well and high in Palm Springs. With a well-developed taste for nose candy, Skip would be a good contact for further distribution in Southern California.

After crossing the border, Sycorax planned to follow the same route that she had taken to Glamis but now west toward the junction with Calexico and route 111 north. She would have to pass the US Border Patrol on either the route 86 west side of the Salton Sea or the east route 111 on the other side of that poisoned lake. Rumor had it that there were some personnel problems on the route 86 side, which would improve her chances of just being waved through without any formal inspection. She'd make the decision on which route to take when she reached Brawley where routes 111 and 86 divided.

Sycorax and Priscilla left the complex late that afternoon nursing hangovers and forgetting to say goodbye to their son and grandson. Juanito was already in school and son and brother Caleb was planting trees for his uncle. Her Lincoln blurted exhaust fumes and dust as it took the mother-daughter team to the US by way of Tijuana and Mexicali. At their departure, Juan Diego opened and closed the heavy, virtually impenetrable door to the complex. He remembered to close the door but forgot to lock it.

Silly, stupid Juan Diego.

***

Antonio could feel it. It was early evening. They all could feel it. He couldn't see anything yet – the cleared fields and cemetery allowed him vision within rifle shot but not beyond. But they – the Mexican Marines and probably Special Agent MacDuff – were out there somewhere and closing in on the compound and on his life.

"*Bad Boyz...Bad Boyz... what you gonna do when they come for you?*" Antonio heard ringing in his ears. He couldn't stop it: His taste ran to classical but even <u>Mozart's Magic Flute</u> couldn't shake the incessant sound of "*Bad Boyz...Bad Boyz...what you gonna do when they come for you?*" He tried classic rock and ranchero but nothing seemed to work.

"*Bad Boyz ...Bad Boyz*" the sound ringing in his ears morphed into "*Bad Boy... Bad Boy...* "Which was what the priest called Antonio when the priest did those bad things to him.

Antonio remembered the priest. The narrow shouldered holy man with doughy white face, girly hips only partially obscured by long shirttails: Short and fat. Poor in sports, but strong in passion. There was no way to avoid him. He controlled food, lodging and his baby brother Stephano.

"Bad boys do bad things – or worse- they make holy men do bad things. I love your brown skin. It's so cool...so smooth. You make me crazy," the priest said. "You make me sin."

The priest usually removed his trousers...but never his clerical collar even under the flowered, rayon shirt he affected during off hours. Sometimes he was in such a rush – busy man had to say mass and hear confessions – that he didn't even bother to drop his pants.

"I hated it," Antonio said to himself. "Mamacita wanted me to be a priest. Dad was killed right before my eyes by a crazed druggie in our bodega. We were totally dependent on our mother church. Statues of Lupita Virgin were everywhere. Why didn't she help."

Antonio never forgot the abuse. It hurt.

"That was when I got my plastic copy of Santa Muerte – her black onyx glow and nihilistic aspect completed the picture – nothing was sure except death," he remembered. "And Santa Muerte was Death's Saint. The Nothingness of death gave me the strength to succeed at my studies and sleep walk through the stuff that the priest did to me."

We Mexicans have a thing about Death," Antonio chuckled to himself. "At least it's certain. And on November 2 Senior Death can be kind of fun. Almost as silly as our thing for big, splashy American cars – I just can't help but love that Escalade."

"Sometimes, I screamed when the nightmares got too close," Antonio remembered. "I even woke up some of my dormitory roommates and had to make excuses. But this Bad Boy never let on ...Even on her deathbed ...I wouldn't let

Mamacita know what I had done – or what had been done to me. I had promised to take care of baby brother Stefano – who had some kind of problem. Some might call it autism but we never had enough money to really find out what his problem was or how to treat it.

"I left the seminary the day Mamacita died."

***

Antonio's interior monologue continued:

"Impossible living an orphaned sixteen year old with a damaged baby brother trying to survive in El Dorado. So I did what I had to do: Seminary training had taught me that I was attractive to older men. Why not make some money at doing what they wanted to do to me; or more often than not, doing those things to them that the priest had done to me."

"Mamacita was the only woman I had ever loved, and I lost her. Dad died before he had the chance to introduce me to ladies of the evening and the ritual of losing my virginity. The physical aspect of loving a woman seemed to be the exclusive province of the rich boys at Seminary who had the time, money and drugs to attract woman of easy virtue."

"It seems that prostitution goes hand in hand with drugs. Ironically but, now with El Simba I am making a living at managing prostitution with a goal of winning the riches of trafficking illegal drugs."

"Some of my clients used drugs. There was money to be made. So as soon as I could, I made the transition from being a male prostitute to acting the life and style of a drug dealer."

From prostitution to drugs: "Muling drugs and even better selling drugs proved a new world for me- an exciting and well-paid enterprise that brought a form of respect and girls...coca and girls go hand in hand ...the more and better the coca...the more and better the girls."

Physical relationships with women were great. Gone was the pain and humiliation of sex in bar room bathrooms or stranger men's bedrooms."

"My first," Antonio remembered with a smile on his face. "My first was an older woman – Mexican and American whose parents had emigrated from someplace in Eastern Europe. Blond. Tall. Wow. Since then, I've never been with better."

"Y Tu Mama Tambien?" With that thought, Antonio's confessional stopped dead. He could remember abuse at the hand of a priest, prostitution, and drug dealing – even treachery and murder which were to come later – but the possibility that he had lost his virginity to Sycorax, Priscilla's mother could not be countenanced.

***

With the sounds of *Bad Boy...Bad Boy* still ringing in his ears, Antonio roused from his reverie to marvel how half a lifetime could be remembered in just a few minutes. He trained his binoculars out his second story office window through the darkening skies to see beyond the cleared fields ... and yes they, the Marines, were out there.... The sound of *"What you gonna do when they come for you..."* came back to his ears.

"I know what I'm going to do when they come for me," Antonio answered the music in his ears. "When I took over this place, built the walls and cleared the fields of fire, I also built a tunnel – far enough and deep enough to escape from this place."

"This place," Antonio thought. "What a wonderful idea El Viejo Filemon had: He was going to provide a place where peasant farmers – los *campesinos* –could get a decent meal and a good clean night's sleep. Rest from their labors and refresh before they moved on to the next field. Don't know where he got the money. Nobodies' money is clean in Sinaloa: Probably a blood debt. But he was very religious – Crucifixes and Lupita Virgins all over the place."

El Viejo Filemonn, Antonio's patron, was fair skinned, shorter than average sporting a fierce mustache and with fore arms bigger and stronger than most men's thighs. He was always dressed to the nines: Sombrero – a five star Texan; new, rhinestone striped Levis 501 and freshly pressed plaid shirt; snakeskin boots; and bling – a thick silver cross that never left his neck. For some reason, he had dispensed with his *achichinques,* the swarm of bodyguards essential for a drug lord. Little was known of his family although it was rumored that El Chapo, Shorty Guzman, who headed up the Sinaloa cartel from a heavily guarded estate in Western Mexico was his son.

"Whatever his background or motivation, El Viejo took me in. He was a stupid...idealistic...crazy old man. I was betwixt and between – dealing drugs was old and the people were dangerous and boring. Didn't really pay all that well either. I needed something different."

"Then from heaven or hell came Priscilla...wild... blond ...blue-eyed...tall...legs that reached all the way to heaven and beyond. Fabulous booty...not much up top, but I rarely got that far. Black knit stockings...wrap up and around and down mini skirt ...Loved danger... Excitement. An American... Gringa with dual citizenship. And, yes, there was also something familiar about her."

"On vacation in Mazatlan, she came to party dangerous in Sinaloa. She showed her appreciation when I gave her that good clean, strong coca. My friends gawked when they met her – she went from nose candy to arm candy. A head taller than me, I would just strut when we were together. Macho needed no telling."

Her appreciation continued when she gave me Juanito. With my wife I lived passion and ambition; with my son I learned love.

Blessed Juanito: Now ten years old growing tall like his mom and brown like me, my son could grow up to be the next Mexican president. He looked great in his private school uniform – white alligator shirt and khaki pants. His hazel eyes betrayed a loving, gentle and sensitive nature, like me, but I have fought my whole life to suppress that side. A bright kid and outstanding soccer player, his grades had fallen recently probably due to living in this environment. Hopefully the old man can help him lift his grades. Maybe sometime I'll be able to send him to boarding school in the United States."

***

"El Viejo Filemon was happy to have me around on a full time basis. Los campesinos came and went with the seasons, but I stayed put and had the time to work and the gift of running things – to do the paper work, pay the bills and make sure the physical plant was in order. El Viejo just wanted everybody fed and happy. Couldn't abide administration."

"Jorge drifted into the complex with a friend – another Jorge. They were different from the other Campesinos– the tattoos gave them away. The Sinaloa Cartel and Los Zetas were just starting to war for control of the drug routes into what had been exclusively Sinaloa territory. Jorge was a Los Zeta scout – his job was to gather intelligence on the situation in Sinaloa and report back to his bosses in Nuevo Laredo. He never denied the Los Zeta connection but insisted his old gang was a thing of the past. We all knew that there is no past with Los Zetas."

"I'd dealt dangerous and criminal," Antonio remembered, "but actual physical violence was not part of me – I would learn how to delegate murder, torture and the other tools of physical enforcement. I needed Jorge: There were times when Los Campesinos would get out of line – a little too much beer or maybe some drug enhanced marijuana. Jorge would straiten them out – break a few teeth in the process, crush a few eggs but got the job done. I looked the other way."

"Working with El Viejo could be very frustrating. The old man meant well but he had no head for business and seemed to spend all his money on clothes. If I ran the place," I figured, "we could turn a profit and improve the physical plant –build some walls, strengthen the entranceway and cut down the corn field to a reasonable size so we could see danger approaching."

"Where does frustration stop and ambition begin ...when does ambition become criminal? I shared these frustrations with Jorge and Priscilla who encouraged my ambition. There were winks ...nods between Priscilla and Jorge which I saw and silently agreed with but chose outwardly to ignore that conversation."

"The next day Jorge reported that El Viejo, the beloved Filemon, had died in his bed – stabbed to death. The murderers knives were on his pillow and still wet with blood.

Damned Campesinos – those drifters couldn't be trusted," he reported. The alleged assassins were quickly disposed of and buried in a common grave.

El Viejo was buried quietly, and I asked no questions. Neither did the El Dorado police. We paid them well. After Filemon, it got easier to live with the rest of the murders that became an every day part of just doing business."

At first, Filemon's death was liberating: I trashed all the Lupita Virgins and crucifixes that were littering the place, improved the physical plant, armed those Campesinos I could trust and made them my soldiers. I quickly reopened my connections in El Dorado and began running local prostitution and drug dealing. Money was coming in: Priscilla got her Bling, we got our Escalade and Juanito got a private school.

But all the bling, Escalades and private schools wouldn't stop the ghosts – those nights when I'd wake up, sweating and screaming - *I never killed anybody* – but the other voice would always come back reminding me that y*ou have murdered many.* I could see Priscilla wandering around in her sleep or out of it just rubbing her hands together and muttering something I couldn't quite hear. Even she, so ambitious for me, must have felt the guilt. "

"As I recall, John Milton's Satan says that he would rather" *rule in hell than serve in heaven.* "Satan was wrong. Better serve in heaven. I now rule in my own little hell and, yes, by every definition, it is truly hell. Given the chance, I would give my soul –that is if I had one unsold – just to clean El Viejo's toilet."

***

"Senior ...senior, I need your advice ...the Marines want to parlay...they'd like to send over Special Agent Malcolm MacDuff of the American FBI to discuss possible conditions for the release of the hostages," Juan Diego implored Antonio.

Roused from reverie and still pursued by the little black dog of depression, Antonio took a while to adjust to this new person calling to him for a decision that could well be a question of life or death.

"Aren't you ...that's right ...Juan Diego? Friends with Jesus. Sorry about Jesus. Nice guy. Bright. His elimination was just a cost of doing business. Shouldn't you be in the yard planting flowers," Antonio questioned the newly minted Juan Diego – the silly, ill-educated farmer with little or no family who now appeared before him standing tall, gun in his belt with an AK 47 at ready.

"No time for flowers," Juan Diego replied. "In this situation, you need soldiers –not gardeners."

"Couldn't agree more. Soldiers. Guns. Bullets. Pain. Torture. Death. It looks like that today we'll worship at the feet of La Santa Muerte and her angel Jesus Mal Verde. No time for pretty flowers," Antonio responded.

"Now, tell the Marines' representative – I guess it's the guy with the white flag – that I need about an hour to get ready. Call Jorge. We have some important business to discuss."

***

"Jorge, today is the day we didn't what to happen but knew would. Looks like plan A: Do something with Caleb – maybe handcuff him to the truck...keep Cerberus tied up ...I don't know where those troublesome wolf dogs are …don't worry about them."

As Antonio was instructing Jorge, the first flash grenade was tossed into the complex followed by the all too potent whiff of tear gas. When he looked out his second story window, Antonio could see that the Marines had cut the remaining corn stalks and were using them as camouflage as they approached. It looked like a whole cornfield was marching on the El Simba complex.

"Now Plan B: If I don't contact you within an hour, kill the hostages. Take Stefano with you. If any of our soldiers chose to go easy on our beloved Marines, kill them too."

***

In the gathering darkness, Special Agent MacDuff crossed the empty cornfield under a white flag of truce. He was alone. Juan Diego opened the people door to the complex and followed the FBI man up to Antonio's office.

"Buenas Tardes Senior Antonio, MacDuff began. "I find it strange and sad that I have to visit you under these circumstances. My prayers had been that on my next trip to Mexico you would be well established as a priest in El Dorado or a nearby village. I'm sorry it has come to this."

"Cut the BS pig," Antonio shot back. "We're here to discuss business. Before you ask, the hostages are well and the price for their release is $1,000,000 – no Benjamin's."

"At risk of appearing rude, how do I know that they are OK? May I speak to them – not to question your word but just to assure myself that their condition is acceptable? Can't pay for damaged good, you know" MacDuff replied.

"Your religion is weird and boring. I could barely stay awake during our discussions that seemed to last all night," Antonio shot back.

"I really don't see what my faith has to do with this situation," MacDuff replied. "I just want to be sure that your charges are alive and in reasonably good health. The old man was diabetic and could suffer if not given his medication."

"Bad Boy...Bad Boy" started screaming in Antonio's ears. The little black dog of depression reminded him of his father's murder, the little bump in his mother's breast that grew to kill her...

"Bad Boy...Bad Boy ...you made me sin...you corrupted a holy man..." said the priest ... "I hate doing this with strange men...who will care for Stefano...I love Juanito... Priscilla has a Sancho ...I made love to her mother Sycorax... No ...no ...I didn't kill Jesus or the others...I've never killed anybody..."

"But you've murdered many," the voices concluded.

"Shut up," Antonio cried to MacDuff. "Just lay it on...we'll see who the real man is..."

With that scream ...the cry from within his battered soul, Antonio pulled the revolver from his shoulder holster, aimed it at MacDuff who was less than six feet away and...

Fired. A loud bang ...smoke and fire...Antonio was mortally wounded. He turned to see his killer ...expecting that Jorge would someday turn on him...but with a puzzled look on his face that was death alive, he saw Juan Diego ...

"This is for my friend Jesus...the innocent man you murdered and I buried...you and your friends laughed about his suffering," Juan Diego told the mortally wounded man.

Juan Diego then ended Antonio's life with a second bullet from his police special – a noisy antiquated weapon that

Jorge had given him assuring that it wouldn't hurt anybody. Juan Diego had learned his army lesson well – he brought down Antonio with two bullets to the body mass: The first punctured his lung and the second was a gut shot. There was blood but not the plethora of blood, bone and brains that would greet the first responders to the sight of victims gunned down by assault weapons.

"Never again ...no more...never ... never...Virgin Mother forgive me. I have sinned," Juan Diego cried and threw down the revolver, which clunked dull noise on the floor.

In the evening light of a second story window in a cement building, Juan Diego's profile shook off the oppressed, ignorant farmer he had been and assumed the Mayan nobility, which he had always been. His features blossomed – regal high cheekbones, his high bridged nose and brown skin showed radiant.

"I owe you my life," MacDuff told the tear stained Juan Diego. "Thank you."

Dead on the floor Antonio's body lay curled in fetal position. His face showed neither rage nor peace but appeared a sign of relief. In heaven, hell, purgatory or in the ether that surrounds all our lives the black dog of depression and the scars of a cursed childhood were finally silent. The Bad Boy slept.

Mijo. And Antonio awoke in that place that stands between before and after time again to the sound of *Mijo* – his mother was calling him to bed where she would tuck him in and say his prayers. Or was that his father, so proud, when he made the first string soccer team. *Mijo,* he said, "you will represent Mexico in the world cup. Soft light, warm breath of summer and fresh smell of afternoon rain filled the time before and after time while Antonio followed the light.

The shades of the corrupt priest, Jorge, Priscilla and Sycorax screamed silently from his visions periphery. He hardly noticed them.

"Bienvenido Mijo," sounded from the light. It was El Viejo Filemon, well dressed as in earthly life, the one person who offered him redemption from a life of crime, ambition and Bad Company. And his first murder victim.

El Viejo...El Viejo. I murdered you. Murder is a mortal sin and I must be punished, Antonio wept to his former benefactor.

"Dry your tears *Mijo*," El Viejo Filemon replied." On earth, I sinned and was punished. As one of the founders of the Sinaloa Cartel, I murdered many myself and was a willing participant in a murderous contest that wastes 15,000 Mexican lives a year. The complex you entered was my feeble attempt at atonement and built on blood money. You can't buy forgiveness; you can only accept the free gift of salvation. Now, even my son El Chapo Guzman has been captured and may spend the rest of his life in an American jail."

"Now, *Mijo,* Come walk with me."

An Aztec Prince died that day.

***

MacDuff released the pistol from Antonio's hand. There were no bullets. The chamber was empty and the safety was still on. He had never killed anyone.

Agent MacDuff could only reflect on Antonio's life and think: "There but for the grace of God go I."

"How could it be otherwise," MacDuff thought. And remembered what he had found out about Antonio's life:

Orphaned at 16. Lost his mother to cancer and his father to a drug-crazed gunman. Abused by a priest. Became a male prostitute and drug dealer. Pleasing older men was all he knew how to do: At seminary, he had excelled in liturgical Latin and Greek and performed well in theology, philosophy, math, history and literature. He was a good soccer player, but not good enough to make money at the game. The seminary did not offer vocational training.

Antonio's only chance for redemption was El Viejo Filemon's good offices, but bad company and ambition murdered him. By then life had mortally wounded his soul.

Agent MacDuff's story was a fortunate journey: Missionaries spreading the good news of the Later Day Saints led his forbears from the harsh winters and landscape of their native Scotland through the dangers of the American prairie to Zion in the American desert. Poor folk, his great great grandfather could only boast one wife.

His mother was a breast cancer survivor, his brother autistic and he himself was born premature but healthy thanks to a successful late term caesarian. Mom and kids survived and prospered. His father led the quiet life of an accountant while devoting his spiritual resources to church and the local Boy Scout troop. Family and church remained solid, enduring pillars of strength.

"If circumstances had been different, would my life have resembled Antonio's" he thought. "Well nigh possible," he answered himself. "I might have been worse – I might have murdered out of greed or sadism without the limitations of Antonio's inhibitions."

As an FBI agent, MacDuff had seen death and, unlike Antonio, had actually killed other human beings. Not many and they were all bad guys. It wasn't fun. But he had killed. Unlike Antonio, however, he had never murdered. "Well, if I murdered, it was by mistake." Or was that what he liked to tell himself.

***

Waking from his dialogue with himself, MacDuff asked Juan Diego about the hostages – where were they and in what condition.

"Senior," Juan Diego informed the Agent, "Patron Antonio told Jorge – his enforcer – that if he didn't tell him of a successful negotiation with you within an hour that he was to kill the hostages and escape through a tunnel he had built for that purpose."

"That was an hour and a half ago," Juan Diego related to MacDuff. "And Jorge is never late."

Juan Diego then waved a white flag of truce to the Mexican Marines who were moving toward the complex and firing sporadically at the remaining narco soldiers who were foolish, brave or stoned enough not to keep their heads down. He mouthed to the soldiers - "it's open. The door is open." Again, Juan Diego had forgotten to lock the door.

***

"I guess, I could've been a wiper man," Jorge said to himself as he led Caleb– hands tied in duck tape behind his back– pistol to the back of his head – to the truck and a pair of handcuffs to keep him tied to the steering wheel for the duration.

"But, on the other hand, wiper man doesn't pay well...no respect. Probably don't live any longer than us narcos," Jorge said to himself as he continued his interior dialog. "Besides, I like what I do – there's a finality about killing people. And respect. Let me tell you about respect – the look in their eyes before they die is nothing but respect. And fear. And power."

Now, Jorge had to gather up Stefano, who with the excitement of the impending Los Marines' assault was crazier than ever. He would have killed Caleb on the spot but felt honor bound to skip that pleasure because of his relationship with Antonio; same with Stefano who just got in the way of business.

Jorge checked his watch and thought: "Nothing from Antonio. Time to make the walk to the end house and kill the hostages. Escape through the tunnel. Don't know where the wolf dogs are – take care of them later. The Marines wouldn't use heavy weapons, but they would have snipers – best to stay low behind the wall."

The Marines lobbed another flash grenade into the complex along with another canister of tear gas. Hunched low with a wet rag contra tear gas covering his face, ears ringing from the grenades and with Stefano in tow, Jorge knew that a fifty-meter walk could last an eternity.

***

"Stay down Stefano," Jorge yelled at his charge. Then a Marine's bullet nipped Stefano's shoulder – a little blood - and he scrunched down and started to cry.

"They hurt me...those bad soldiers made me bleed," Stefano complained to nobody in particular. "Die ... bad soldiers...die." he screamed and raised his body above the wall and fired blindly into the cornfield.

The next sniper's bullet found its mark and Stefano died instantly. Jorge stepped over the body and muttered "crazy retard" and continued on his mission. Jorge was not noted for political correctness.

***

Without Stephano to worry about, Jorge continued his progress toward the hostages. He walked head down to thwart snipers bullets and wet rag held against his face to reduce the potency of the tear gas. And Jorge remembered:

"Sin numbre...sin numbre...no name...no name...it doesn't matter ...nobodies' got a name here...best not to have one."

"You don't want the soldiers knowing your name. When they come to kill the guerillas – just hide in the forest and try not to hear your women being raped or your men being murdered."

Somewhere hidden in the forest outside his village in Guatemala, Jorge lost his soul to survival needs and bloodlust.

The Mexican Marines threw another flash grenade over the wall's concertina wire and their sniper fire continued to keep him crouched down sheltered only by the a concrete wall six inches thick and one meter high.

"I've got to keep my mind on business," he thought to himself. "If I don't, I'll get killed before I get to the hostages – just like that idiot Stephano."

But his mind wandered back anyway- back to Guatemala where the white people lived in the cities and spoke Spanish, and where the hill people, descendants of a great pre-Columbian empire, spoke Mayan, his first language.

The gangs had little problems enlisting killers to enforce the dominance of one Mexican Cartel over the other. While losing up to 15,000 thugs a year, the Cartels were running out of Mexicans and needed to look to the failing states- Honduras, El Salvador and Guatemala- of Central America for fresh blood.

"I didn't care much either way," Jorge thought to himself as he dodged another bullet and tried to cough the tear gas out of his lungs. "Better to be a killer than to be killed and wait around, listen to your people being massacred and hide in the trees until it was your turn to die. It was easy to learn Spanish and I can field strip an AK 47 as well as any Mexican Marine."

"A lot of people died when they tried to cross the bridge and river border into Mexico," he recalled. "But with gang protection we could count on relatively safe passage across the border and onto the Beast – the long train ride north. People got killed on the train too, but not us. We had protection."

Boasting neither a living mother nor father, orphaned Jorge survived on what food his little village could share with him and what he could steal. Dark skinned, short and powerfully built, the adult Jorge resembled a cement block walking. He limped courtesy of a Mexican Marine bullet to his left leg and the less than professional ministrations by a cartel doctor.

The scars, the tattoos and the ultimate M 13 would come later- a product of cartel lifestyle and personal choice.

Nobody knew if Jorge was born ugly or got that way through the efforts of a soldier's rifle butt. His dark face was caved in with his nose, which resembled a pig's snout, crushed up somewhere between his beady black eyes while his jug ears stared back at this face in apparent alarm. The scraggly beard and spotty mustache only enhanced his bleak appearance. Women did not come easily –when he had money, he paid for love; when he was broke, he took it.

His cartel nickname, El Sapo, the Toad, came before his name Jorge which he took along with the life of his first target, another 13 year old, who was caught stealing from the cartel. As a cartel soldier, he could expect to die before 25. He didn't know exactly when he was born, but he knew time was running out.

He was almost there now. He dropped some more meth and washed it down with a slug of tequila. He planned to kick in the door to their room, spray the area with a full clip from his AK47 and take care of anything that might still be living with his pistol and knife.

***

"It can't be," Jorge thought as he looked through the mist of tear gas and the crash of grenades and approached the hostage's living space.

He had a vision of a giant on horseback who was poking a rusty old lance at him and threatening to unman him through some strange and unfamiliar rite.

The whole conversation was spoken in English with some very strange sounding words from a foreign language. Jorge understood what the Spector was saying and replied to the vision:

***

"Halt Knave."

This order crowded out the noise of flash grenades and the rat-tat tat of rifle shots. Atop his rearing power horse, Rosy, nostrils flaming fire (the horse) and fully eight feet high (the man), a blinding vision out of the gloom of tear gas and early nightfall appeared to Jorge and said:

"I, Don Ariel Rabinowitz, of Brooklyn, Bed Sty Section, knight of many problems and severe intestinal distress, order you – yea you, Jorge you ugly toad – I know your nickname - to stop your progress, make confession, cease your evil ways and return to Guatemala. Obey or, in the name of my fair Emilinea, you will feel the bite of my Toledo steel."

"Look here mashugana, you got it all wrong," Jorge shouted back at the looming specter of Don Ariel Rabinowitz, our faithful knight and champion. "I read the book."

"The name is Quixote and you're from La Mancha in Spain."

"You got trouble wit Brooklyn", thundered Don Ariel Rabinowitz. "You wouldn't last five minutes in Bed Sty. Rabinowitz? Dat's an honored and noble name. Now shut up and stop rattling the china or you will feel the bite of my Toledo steel."

"That thingy – yea the wooden pole with the rusty old iron tip glued to it is a lance. Yea, putz, a lance like the weapon you used against the windmills. The thing you're threatening me with. Toledo steel is your sword."

"OK, schlepper, technology is not my long suite," responded our saving knight and chivalrous hero. "I'll go that one for you. But I doubt you've had your bris. In my hands, the sword could do the job. I'll be your Moyle. Cut or uncut?"

"Uncut and I want to stay that way," replied Jorge.

"Oh, Bubblelh, it won't hurt," soothed our fair knight. "From what I hear from the bunkhouse, your whole thing is no big deal. It'll just be a little operation. In your case, a very little operation, and your appearance will improve dramatically. After the procedure we'll have a nice party: matzo ball soup, latkes, a lot of sour cream ...Manachevitz wine... you know the whole real deal."

"Maybe you could make some new friends. Some lady friends. Nice girls. The kind your Mom would have approved of – oops sorry, you didn't have a Mom – or none who would claim you. And "Who's your Daddy. Must be a bird," our fair knight continued.

"Or maybe you're a little more DC than AC?"

With the mention of romantic preference, Jorge recalled a time in prison and that beautiful blue-eyed blond haired boy. Was it memory or fantasy? Whatever the reality of the experience, fantasy or memory, Jorge put the thought away and continued to deal with this presence that continued to taunt him.

"Enough of this," Jorge shot back at our dyspeptic hero, "Look here schlimazel, your horse's name is Rocinante and you do your business for the Fair Dulcinea."

"You've gone too far now, schmuck," our fair night replied. "Rosy is my horse's nickname. We're together a lot and I don't feel like we should stand on formalities. I don't know from no Dulcinea. I do what I do in the name of my fair Emilinea – Caleb's math teacher and one serious Babe."

"You called me a schmuck and that's a bad word," cried the wounded and sensitive Jorge.

"Oy, sensitive goyem. Now calm down sissy, man up and be a mensch. Sticks and stones ...you know the drill.

"And besides that Buba" our disputatious Don continued. "The word schmuck is derived from the German word for jewelry. It's Yiddish. Pretty clever don't you think?"

"Yiddish ...Shmiddish," Jorge replied. "You called me a bad name and for that you disappear." Jorge opened fire. Emptied the full clip of his AK 47 into the image of our Fair Knight.

The bullets clattered harmlessly against the concrete walls. He then threw down his empty weapon and crashed through the door armed with only a knife and his prized Glock.

***

Bullets flying all over the place. Tuma and I had gone to Dad and Mom's room to escape the stink of tear gas and crushing noise of those horrible flash grenades. You know how sensitive we dogs are to smell and noise.

"Not to get shot at," I complained as a bullet came crashing through our door – one winged it through the window and almost hit me – the Queen does not take kindly to being shot at.

So, Mom and Dad and Tuma and I did what we could with our hands, paws and noses to repel the murderous thug Jorge. We pushed what little furniture we had, boxes and whatever against the door. Our most considerate captures had neglected to fit with a lock.

I knew it was that thug Jorge. Swearing like a devil, he pushed and shoved and broke though our defenses. Once inside our room, he raised his gun to fire.

Lightening struck.

I grabbed his arm, tore into it with my wolf teeth, broke the ligaments above his wrist and crunched down on the bones and arteries of his lower arm. His prized Glock went flying, free from his murderous grip.

Thunder roared.

A split second later, Tuma – eyes flashing red, ears thrown back… teeth dripping blood – threw down the thug…ripped through his forward carotid arteries, crushed his windpipe and cracked the bones in his neck…

More death rattle than conscious thought, Jorge pulled the knife from his boot and thrust it into Tuma's gut – piercing the peritoneum and slicing through his aorta. Tuma was dying …my hero…my friend was dying…a friend who, given the chance, I would have died for myself.

I did what I could for Tuma. I licked his wounds ….I put my head on his quivering body …I even punched him a little like I used to when we'd flirt. Nothing.

Tuma was dead. I mourned for all the dead wolves …all the alpha males killed by human assassins …all my brothers and sisters abandoned and murdered in shelters. I howled to heaven and snarled down to hell. I cried my Kaddish until…

I felt a soft warm hand behind my ears…a gentle voice called to me. I looked up and saw Officer Ariel Rabinowitz, US Border Patrol, whispering to me from John 15:13: "Greater love has no one than this, that he lay down his life for his friends."

Yes, Tuma had sacrificed his life for me, his friend. He didn't even know my humans. He lost his life for my sake, for my quest.

As Officer Ariel Rabinowitz faded into the ether, he reminded me, "Tend to your humans. Tuma is mine now."

***

"Where are the police when you need them," I thought when Special Agent MacDuff, FBI, and Captain Beltran, the Marines, finally arrived in our room – the scene of murder and mayhem only a few minutes before.

"It looks like the dogs got him when he knocked down the door and crashed into the room," Mexican Marine Captain Beltran said to FBI Special Agent MacDuff as they looked at Jorge's torn remains.

"I think the small dog tore the gun from his hand, Captain Beltran continued, "and then the big dog knocked him down and gutted him."

"That's not a pretty site," Agent MacDuff observed.

"Jorge never was a pretty site," Captain Beltran concluded.

***

"Typical of humans," I thought: "First they're late and then take credit for the sacrifice we dogs have made. I don't know why we put up with them. On the other hand, they do give super tummy rubs and good food – a combination which goes a long way toward my tolerance of their species."

Tuma – at cost of his own life -and I – at extreme inconvenience -had dispatched that thug Jorge. Credit? Do we get credit? For bravery? For loyalty? Well, at least my humans were safe and I could take care of them without the issues of thugs, guns, noisy explosions and smelly tear gas.

I overheard Agent MacDuff tell Captain Beltran how lucky we had been: Upon entering the compound, Agent MacDuff had seen Jorge, at a distance and through the swirl of smoke and tear gas, arguing vehemently with something or somebody.

"Yes, Captain Beltran replied. "I saw it too. I know that there was smoke and tear gas, but when I looked at Jorge – oh he must have been 50 meters away – it was like I was looking up from underwater –clear but kind of swirly."

"I observed the same kind of thing," Agent MacDuff said. "Now, did you hear something like a person speaking a foreign language or English with a strong foreign accent?

"Copy that," Captain Beltran said. "They call it the fog of war – it's hard to recall what really happened with the adrenalin hissing through your veins and death and smoke and stink and noise crashing in on all your senses. But I agree that there was something odd...otherworldly... about the whole scene."

"Whatever it was," Agent MacDuff concluded. "But just think that if Jorge had opened fire with his AK47 on automatic he would have been able to kill the old couple, the dogs and even the houseplant. Instead of that, he spent his entire magazine shooting into the air and using up all his ammunition. He crashed through the door with only a pistol and a knife. And met his fate at the fangs of two dogs."

"That knife killed Tuma" I remembered.

"Funny thing about that houseplant – a cactus –I believe," Captain Beltran smiled. "I heard from Caleb that the last time he went to the old couples room, the cactus was wearing a pair of Victoria Secret's underwear. Like they say, "there may be snow on the roof but fire in the furnace."

"Well, in regard to the old couple, that reminds me," Agent MacDuff said, "I have to fill my prescription for Viagra."

Captain Beltran and Agent MacDuff ended their conversation and went to complete their paperwork. You can't even die without filling in some official form.

April 3, Coachella

A few days later, more news: Sycorax made it past the Mexicali East Gate to Glamis and route 111 north to La Quinta where she chose to chance the west-side Salton Sea Border Patrol station. Captain Gutierrez had taken over from Officer Mount, who needed one of many potty breaks – prostate issues I guess – when he found contraband in Sycorax' big black Lincoln.

Captain Gutierrez called to Officer Mount, who was just emerging from the bathroom, to apprehend the alleged drug smuggler. Mount ran to the government issue SUV, mounted up and gave chase to Sycorax who had taken off in a cloud of dust and exhaust smoke toward Coachella.

At the intersection of route 86 and 111, near the agricultural town of Mecca, Officer Mount rolled and totally destroyed the SUV and seriously injured himself as well. Upon hearing news of the accident, Captain Gutierrez breathed a sigh of relief and thought – "Officer Mount can now go on permanent disability – the paperwork will be much easier than actually firing that incompetent."

Reymundo Ortiz, Sheradino's friend and Coachella Police Chief, later arrested Sycorax following a routine traffic stop.

***

El Dorado, March 31

One of the soldiers released Caleb and Cerberus. Our friend Cerberus barked, "Sorry, we missed the party, but we were all tied up. Get it –all tied up to the truck and with some chain buried in the ground. Like, we were all tied up." Cerberus just loves puns. I groaned appropriately.

Caleb then apologized to my humans for his inability to help them in their struggles with the narcos: Same for Cerberus who was most happy to be with Caleb, his new human. "Every dog needs a boy," our fierce pit bull thought.

***

"You've got a lot of ground to make up and cover," Agent MacDuff told Caleb. "The story you made up about some money that Dad and Mom were supposed to have won- the ransom demands and kidnapping that followed almost got them killed. Plus you've got a history of petty thefts and armed robbery. You've straightened up since you found out the realities of the world of narco traficantes, but you still need to do a lot more work before your slate will be cleaned… more than just a short finger to remind you.

"I can help out with that problem," Juan Diego chipped in. "It's all come very soon, but it looks like I'll be in charge here for a while. The paperwork on ownership of this complex was never fully clear so the Mexican government has taken control of this property and put me in charge. I'll make Caleb my ward. I'll need some help, but I understand that Agent MacDuff has some co-religionists around who can pitch in."

"And we can help out with Juanito who has suddenly become an orphan." Agent MacDuff offered. "Similar to Caleb's situation, sometimes family values are not the best answer: Sycorax will be seeing jail time and at best Priscilla will be on probation – Antonio is dead. I'll also be looking into a wonderful American couple who would make great parents – if they'd only agree to take the final step of adoption."

Funeral detail soon arrived. They'd already bagged up three nameless thugs –*sin nombres*- as well as Stefano and Antonio. Six dead if you include Jesus – pretty small potatoes in the 15,000 dead a year in the Mexican drug wars. There were also another five captives who were headed for prison and one who had apparently escaped.

"Wow," the detail's sergeant said in disbelief. "That dead guy looks like he was attacked by a pack of wolves. I'm surprised that they didn't eat him. Maybe they would have if there were enough time."

"That was a pack of two," Dad replied.

"But where's Tuma's body," Mom observed. "Courage is a tough little gal – she struck at the thug like lightening and disarmed him, but Tuma thundered in and killed him."

"Yes, where is Tuma, my hero dog ... the dog who gave his life to save innocents," I said. His body was nowhere to be found.

"Where ...where ...I kept thinking ..." and then I looked at the cactus.

I wagged my tail...and looked again ...and wagged my tail again.

And, you know what?

The cactus smiled.

Chapter 6. The Cactus Smiled Part 2. *El Dorado to Tijuana and from Tijuana to the East Mexicali-Calexico Border Crossing.*

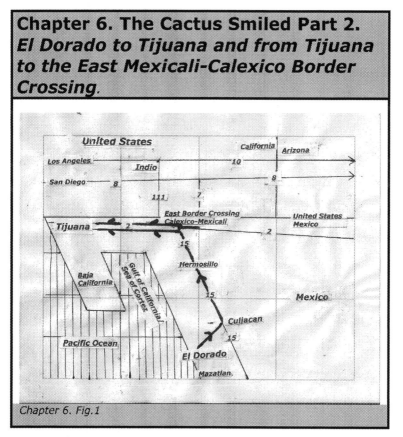

Chapter 6. Fig. 1

Sycorax first drove to Tijuana where she picked up the goods and then drove parallel to the US border where she offloaded the goods which were muled in an under border tunnel where she could pick them up for distribution in Glamis and points north.

Chapter 6. The Cactus Smiled Part 2. *Mexicali to Brawley to Glamis to Brawley to Coachella.*

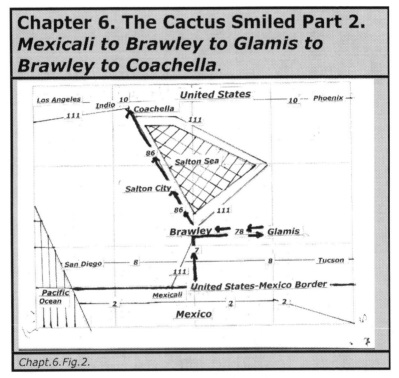

Chapt.6.Fig.2.

Sycorax offloaded the goods on the Mexicali side of the East Gate where a mule took them under the gate to the American side. At the Rt.86 Border Patrol Station, Officer Mount gave chase and crashed his vehicle. In Coachella Captain Ortiz stopped her at a traffic light and discovered the contraband.

AN EPILOGUE

"OK. Calm down Courage. I'm coming. I'm coming. Be there in a minute..."

Those were his last words.

We lost Courage almost five years ago ... let's see ...that would be back in 2018, and we just lost the old man.

The old man told Courage to "calm down" and "I'm coming" any number of times as he woke ...even after she died. I guess it was habit. When she was with him, she'd jump in bed, snuggle with Mom and then push him out of bed. Then pester him while he dressed for their morning walk.

Mom tried to bring the old man around but to no avail. He just seemed to lose his life when he lost Courage. I guess you could say he lost his courage when he lost his Courage. Mom even bought him a new dog: A nice male – of indefinite heritage. But it was never the same. I guess he was just a one-dog man.

Oh me, yes. You might remember me from our great adventure. I'm Cerberus. The fierce Pit Bull who met his match and more when he encountered Courage and Tuma on that fateful day 13 years ago back in Sinaloa. I followed Caleb to the United States when he joined Job Corps and found a permanent home with the Rodriguez family here in Indio.

We all remember Courage —beautiful, willful, charming and witty – the whole complex mourned her passing. But too few remember Tuma – the true hero dog who gave his life for his friend. I guess, in human talk, you'd call him a mensch, but for us dogs he was a wolf. He was a true wolf who brought surpassing honor to his pack and his heritage.

Things are getting a bit fuzzy for me – going on 15 – what's that – 85 in human years. Even the Jeden is a new bud...a new angel ...but still addicted to beans.

So I'll bark goodbye, but always remember what Courage told us:

"Be still and smell the wind. God's in it."

ABOUT THE AUTHORS

They met in class in 1997: Webb was her ESL teacher and Francisca his student. Fresh from a U. of Maine MS and Peace Corps, Webb - a New Yorker, Columbia AB - publishing brat and newly minted educator arrived in California to survive  on adjunct teaching and book royalties. They both moved to the Coachella Valley in 1995 - he to Palm Springs and she from Mexicali to Indio. Born in Sinaloa, Francisca grew up in Mexicali and has worked as a cleaning lady, a field worker and in retail with Costco.

Married in 2006, they now live in Indio, the heart of the Coachella Valley located about 100 miles north of the border with Mexico and only a few miles from La Frontera - a second border and gate to people and drugs moving north and guns and money moving south. Webb and Francisca cross back and forth on the border to visit Mexicali a few times a month and San Felipe, Gulfo de Santa Clara and Sinaloa yearly. Their dog Courage, a beautiful Siberian Husky, serves as narrator in the quest to save her humans held hostage in the dark heart of Sinaloa. Our hero dog was a birthday present.